ALL THE SCARS OF HOPE

NISSA HARLOW

NIMBLE HOPE PUBLISHING

ISBN: 978-1-7781397-9-6

Published in Canada by Nimble Hope Publishing
Cover and book design by Nissa Harlow

*For those who stick with you
all the way to the end.*

CHAPTER 1

WITHOUT A MAP

Walking through the Rift Zone with a full backpack was probably a stupid thing to do. But I didn't care anymore. I had to survive in this hellhole, and that meant taking risks.

It also meant making hard decisions.

C-Roy had promised me that Click and I could stay with him, no strings attached. But I couldn't. Every time I walked into that kitchen, the memory came rushing back. I couldn't set foot in there without hearing that runner's words echoing about the space. My heart would ache so bad that I felt like I was going to throw up, and I'd have to rush from the room. Buddy would inevitably find me cowering in the living room, curled up on the couch in a haze of anguish, and then Click would spend half an hour mangling my name and trying to coax me back into reality.

So, as much as I might've wanted to stay where the

food was (even though I hadn't been able to force myself to eat much in days), I simply couldn't. And since Click wouldn't stay without me, that was how we ended up walking along the soaked streets a week after . . .

No. My mind wouldn't go there.

Or maybe I just couldn't let it go there.

It had rained every day since. The days hung grey above our heads like harbingers. Except the horrible thing had already happened, so those harbingers were empty threats.

Buddy was going to need a bath. The grit clung to his sodden, white undercarriage as he trotted along the street ahead of us, glancing back occasionally to make sure Click was still there. I was nothing but chopped liver, though I was pretty sure the dog wouldn't have turned up his nose at any sort of liver, chopped or otherwise. It didn't really bother me; I was used to dogs not caring much about my existence. Floyd, Grandpa's one-eyed mongrel, had been a one-man sort of dog, even though I'd fed him about half the time. I'd just been a walking food dispenser as far as he was concerned. Grandpa had been the bearer of chin scratches and cuddles. He was the one who'd held Floyd on his last day. He was the one who'd buried him in the backyard in the shade of the massive rhododendron that Grandma had nicknamed Lord Hulkington.

When we crossed into Ryver's territory, I led us away from Main Street so we could follow a side street that ran parallel. Click glanced at me a few times, as if he wanted to ask why we weren't going straight back to the vet clinic. But he didn't stop me, and he didn't try to say anything. I wasn't entirely sure of my reasons myself, but I suspected that most of it had to do with those first few minutes . . . when I would have to tell Dr. Bryan what had happened. I couldn't bear the thought of it, so I kept us well away from the clinic and any necessity for telling the story.

Joshua's territory was a long, thin shaft of land that ran from the west side of Kenyonville, penetrating right through the midline of the town until it ran up against Niesha's old turf. *A giant dick ruled by a giant dick*, I thought, but even that didn't make me smile. I was too focused on what was beyond his territory. My armpits started to sweat just thinking about it.

We don't have a choice. Well . . . we did. It was just that the other choices weren't great. I didn't want to go grovelling to Xavi. Ryver was out. I'd burned my bridges with Joshua; besides, I didn't want to work for a guy who would eat a pet dog. Rasputin . . . I didn't even consider it. C-Roy was probably the least offensive option, but I couldn't do it. So I just led Click and Buddy north, feeling my stomach sink with every footstep.

It started to spritz a little, the rain falling like mist. The trees in the distance—up in Niesha's old territory—were obscured by the low-hanging clouds. The air felt like a spa treatment (or, what I imagined one might have felt like), and it felt delicious on my newly healed skin. I tilted my chin up, letting the mist fall along my jawline. Out of the corner of my eye, I saw Click step closer. I quickly turned my head away.

"It's fine," I said.

"Lee-ah."

I shook my head and kept walking. He didn't try to stop me. I knew he wanted to do another healing session. The burn on my face had been deep. Really deep. But Click's healing touch seemed to have worked wonders. A glance in the mirror before our departure had shown me that the burn was almost completely healed. Regret had swamped me, thinking of another burn that had gone untreated. And then I just thought about *him*, and that hurt my heart all over again.

There was a lot I didn't know about Click and his time in Kenyonville. And now that I was really curious, there was no one else around to ask. Slowly, I turned my head to look at him, only to find that he seemed to have been waiting for me to do just that. He gave me a little smile, and I turned away again.

"We'll have to figure something out," I mumbled. "We need a way to communicate."

Out of the corner of my eye, I saw him lift his hand to give me a thumbs up. I smiled a little before I could stop myself.

"You understand pretty much everything I say, don't you?"

His thumb, still in the air, wiggled a little in answer.

"You could *try* talking to me. Surely, if you can understand English, you could speak it."

He said nothing. When I glanced at him, I saw a strange expression on his face. It wasn't quite a frown, but it didn't look like a smile, either. It might've been confusion. Or frustration. I really couldn't tell . . . which confused and frustrated *me.*

"Okay. Repeat after me: Yes."

He dropped his hand to his side and stared at me like I was nuts.

"You can't just keep giving me thumbs ups forever."

His eyebrows rose slightly, as if to say, "Why the hell not?"

I sighed. He was right, really. "Fine. Then we'll have to come up with some other hand signs. I hate feeling like I'm talking to myself all the time."

He stepped closer and slipped his hand into mine. For a moment, I was taken aback, not sure what to do. My first thought was that he was trying to make a move on me, and I almost yanked my hand away. Following quickly after that was annoyance and shame, and a flash of understanding. I gave his hand a squeeze.

"Sorry," I said. "I know you're just trying to be kind. It's just . . . I have history with C-Roy, and being in his house again brought up all sorts of . . . stuff."

"See-rah."

"Yeah. Don't worry about him. We're not going back there."

He gave me a thumbs up with his free hand. I grunted in amusement.

"Who taught you that, anyway?"

"Vee-kah."

I swallowed hard. My feet scuffed to a stop as my vision became a blurry mess. I just stood there, breathing hard, trying to keep from bursting into tears. Click slipped his hand out of mine. The next thing I knew, his arms were around me. I threw my arms around him and closed my eyes, resting my chin on his shoulder as I tried to compose myself. A moment later, I heard dog toenails on the asphalt as Buddy approached. Quickly pulling away, I swiped the few tears that had managed to escape and looked down at the dog. He stared up at Click, his expression hopeful. His tail gave an uncertain little wag.

"I bet he's hungry."

"Bah-dee," Click called softly, crouching down and holding out his hand. Buddy came close and sort of nuzzled his head against Click's knee, almost like a cat. It was hard to tell if the scruffy dog was getting skinnier or not. He was probably hungry, though. And, given his history, I didn't want him to get *too* hungry.

"Let's go," I said. "The sooner we get there, the sooner we can eat."

Click gave Buddy's ears a scratch and stood up. Then he reached for my hand again. I grasped it gratefully as we resumed our trek, heading into our uncertain future.

—

spotted the pink line half a block before we reached it. It must've been touched up at some point, because it almost looked like it was doubled, plus it was quite bright. I wasn't sure how well spray paint fared on asphalt, especially over a couple of years of rain, snow, and the baking summer sun.

My heart started to beat a little faster. Of course, I'd seen the line before. I'd even crossed it. But something about seeing that neon slash get closer and closer made me feel like screaming. And running. So I kept a tight grip on Click's hand.

The line ran right down the middle of Bower Avenue. At the corner, I pulled Click onto the sidewalk that ran down one side of the street, the side that was still in Joshua's territory. The houses looked the same as I remembered from years earlier. In fact, the neighbourhood seemed to have fared pretty well. Most of the houses on Joshua's side of the line were adorned with fluttering pink tickets. The lawns were overgrown, though, leading to a less-than-lived-in look. It was hard to tell whether the buildings were actually occupied, or if they'd just been ticketed as some sort of buffer at the edge of the territory. I didn't see any people . . . though that didn't mean they weren't there.

Buddy seemed pretty relaxed as we started down Bower, trotting ahead of us with his tail held high, but after a block or two, he started to slow and look back at Click with uncertainty. He was obviously feeling *my* distress, because Click seemed fine. The only reason the dog would've had to be nervous would've been if he'd known whose turf we were walking through. I doubted he was *that* smart.

We crossed Bay Street and continued down the sidewalk. My steps got slower and slower. Click adjusted his pace to match mine, not reacting to anything in particular, but just trusting my leadership. Buddy fell back, too, until he was walking right beside Click's leg. By the time we stopped, I felt like I was going to pass out.

Maybe this isn't the best idea. I'm triggering all sorts of stuff. Will I really be able to live . . . ?

I turned and looked across the street. I didn't know what I was expecting. Maybe a gaping portal to hell. Windows that looked like eyes. But all that was there was the familiar house, its blue siding faded and grungy, its windows glinting with reflections. The curtains in the second-floor windows were closed, just the way I'd left them two years earlier. The front doorframe was free of tickets, but the door was closed. For some reason, that made me feel a little better, even though I had no idea what we were going to find on the other side.

I looked at Click, and he turned to me with an expectant smile.

"You know where we are, don't you?" I asked.

"Lee-ah," he said, turning back to stare at the house across the street.

"That's right. Welcome to my home." I swallowed hard and looked down at the dog, who had just sat down to vigorously scratch at the side of his neck. "*Our* home," I corrected myself. "Don't you dare infest it with fleas."

CHAPTER 2

DUNCAN AND TASHA'S HOUSE

'd long since lost the key, though I wouldn't have needed it anyway. When I'd abandoned the house, I'd left the door unlocked, reasoning that I didn't want anyone to break the narrow windows on either side to try to gain access. Those windows appeared to be intact. I was sure that someone had been in there in the two years since . . . but if there was no pink ticket now, they were probably gone. Still, that didn't mean things were going to be all sunshine and rainbows on the other side of that door. Abandoned houses tended to get used as toilets.

Honestly. What was wrong with people?

As I stepped off the sidewalk and onto the street, I kept a tight hold on Click's hand, more for reassurance than anything else, because he didn't seem reluctant to cross the street. He was probably curious to see where I had once lived.

I was pretty damn curious to see the place, too.

Crossing the pink painted line felt sort of anticlimactic. I wasn't sure what I'd been expecting. A siren? A hail of bullets from a machine gun mounted across the street? Shaking my head at the thought, I kept my gaze on the door as we drew closer. Kenyonville didn't have any machine guns. At least, it didn't have any that I knew of. And, given some of the kids' fascination with weapons of all kinds, we probably all would've known about any machine guns within the Rift Zone . . . even if they were just being used for target practice with empty bean cans.

As we walked up the front sidewalk and porch steps, I started to relax a little. The house hadn't been entered in a while. Not if the state of the porch was anything to go by. It was filthy with undisturbed grime. Grandma would've been appalled. I could almost hear her voice, telling me to grab the broom and get to work. *Believe me, Grandma. I will. If the broom's still here.*

Buddy sniffed at the bottom edge of the closed door, but didn't react strongly one way or the other. I took that as a good sign. Still, I let go of Click's hand so I could push some Rift energy through my fingertips. I was the only Rifter in the group now, and I felt a sort of responsibility to keep all of us safe. Glancing at Click, I held the index finger of my non-flaring hand to my lips. He gave me a thumbs up. So I grasped the door handle and pressed my thumb down on the lever.

It felt the way I remembered, a little stiff at the beginning, then clunking as the motion completed. Taking a deep breath, I pushed on the door. It swung into the front hall. The house let out a breath of stale air. But it didn't smell as bad as I'd feared. It mostly smelled like a building that hadn't had much airflow for a couple of years.

Buddy didn't even wait for an invitation. He trotted inside, nose down and sniffing vigorously. He could probably smell Floyd's presence, even years later. Especially since our dog had accidentally peed on the floor a few times in his old age.

Click and I stood just inside the front door. I didn't know what he was doing, but I was listening, watching the pink energy flicker silently over my hand. I didn't *hear* anything, but that didn't mean I could get complacent. Someone might've been hiding.

"I'm going to check things out," I whispered. Click turned to me, eyebrows raised. "You want to come with me or stay here?"

"Lee-ah," he said, his voice a rusty whisper as if he wasn't used to trying to keep it so quiet. Nodding, I pushed the front door closed, but not quite all the way. If we had to make a quick escape, I didn't want to have to deal with the tricky latch. Then I stepped farther into the dim space. I'd turned off all the lights before leaving, except for the one at the top of the stairs, but I doubted that incandescent bulb would've still been giving off any light. Grandpa had gradually been switching over to LED bulbs as the incandescent ones had burned out, but that one on the landing had proven to be stubborn. Not quite stubborn enough, though; when I approached the stairs and peered upward, I could see that the second floor was dark.

I passed the staircase and headed toward the kitchen at the back of the house, bypassing the door that hid the basement stairs. I was *not* looking forward to going down there, but I supposed I would have to at some point. The washer and dryer were there (unless someone had hauled them up the narrow stairs, which was unlikely), along with a cache of homemade canned goods. I didn't hold out much hope that Grandma's pickles and corn relish were still on their shelves, though.

The kitchen was dim, being on the north side of the house. But it was bright enough that I could see it looked pretty decent. Many of the cupboard doors were open, so someone had probably done a search, but they were intact. The fridge was still there, buzzing. I would have to brace myself before I opened *that.*

Click went to the back door and pushed aside the curtain so he could peer out into the yard. Buddy, seeming to understand what the door led to, trotted over and scratched at the frame. I shook my head.

"Don't let him out."

Click turned to me, eyebrows raised.

"There's . . . stuff buried in the backyard."

His eyes went a little wider, as if in surprise, even though there was no way he could've possibly known what I meant. I went and joined him at the window to survey the overgrown yard. Lord Hulkington was massive, seemingly trying to take over the entire space. The lower branches, which Grandma had always trimmed back, hung against the ground, so I couldn't see what (if anything) might have been dug up. My gaze drifted over to the other side of the yard, to what had once been the vegetable garden. For a moment, my heart stuttered as I saw the flat ground, and horrible thoughts swirled through my mind.

"Lee-ah," Click said, resting his hand on my arm. I shook him off, just barely missing touching him with my flaring pink hand. I pulled back the energy, my heart pounding.

"It's fine," I said, turning away from the window. "Just let me check the yard before you let him out there, okay? In the meantime, he can pee out front." My throat was tight as I hurried away, heading for the basement stairs. *Be logical,* I reminded myself. *It's been more than two years. The ground will have settled. Besides, if someone had gone digging around in the garden, there would be an obvious hole. Right?* "Right," I whispered. "Right."

"Lee-ah."

"I'm going to check the basement. You coming?"

He followed me, staying a few steps back as I opened the door and reached inside for the light switch. Something tickled my hand, and I pulled back with a yelp, just as a rather large spider fell to the floor and scurried down the hallway. Buddy immediately went after it, sniffing.

"Leave it," I said, but the dog ignored me. I turned to Click. "He's your dog."

He just gave me a thumbs up. I sighed and turned back to the stairwell. Checking carefully to make sure I wasn't about to sweep my head through a spider-web, I stepped onto the small landing and started down the stairs.

The LED lights were cold, but they lit up the space adequately, showing me that it looked pretty much as it should have. The washer and dryer sat against a roughed-in wall, looking like they hadn't been touched. I lifted the lid on the washer, bracing myself for an unpleasant surprise. But the machine was empty. So was the dryer. When I turned the dial and gave the start button an experimental push, the machine rumbled to life. So I checked the washer, too.

"Thank god," I muttered. "At least we can do some laundry." I turned to find Click sort of hugging himself. "Not you, too. What is it with teenage guys and their aversion to soap?"

He didn't answer, but just kept his arms protectively over his fancy shirt. At least, that was what I assumed he was protecting. The denim jacket didn't look worth saving.

Buddy, having finished his adventure with the spider, carefully made his way down the basement steps, nails clicking. I headed for the cabinet in the corner, the one Grandpa had built for Grandma when she'd taken up canning. Finding anything had been a long shot, so I wasn't surprised when I pulled open the door and found the cabinet mostly empty. There were still some supplies—empty glass jars, lids, and blank labels—but all the food was gone. Disappointment sank like a stone into my stomach. I didn't realize how much I'd really wanted a pickle.

"Well," I said, trying to keep my voice brighter than was warranted, given the circumstances, "at least we have the washer and dryer. And there's still the rest of the house to check."

Click let go of himself with one hand to give me a thumbs up, so I headed back to the stairs and started up them. My legs felt like lead (probably because I was half starved), and by the time I got back to the main floor, they were shaking. I made my way to the bottom of the main staircase, keeping a wary lookout for that spider. But I didn't see it. It had probably scurried into a hole. Or Buddy had eaten it. I couldn't really blame him at that point.

The stairs creaked as I pulled myself up them, leaning heavily on the railing. The narrow hallway at the top was dark, being windowless, but I knew the layout well enough that I didn't need to engage my hands for illumination. Pushing open the door to my grandparents' room, I took a step inside.

I could still smell Grandma's soap, even though

she'd been gone for years. The scent lingered in the air like a ghost. I almost expected her to step into view, fiddling with the cuffs of her fine-gauge cardigan that she wore even when the weather was stinking hot. But the room was silent and free of actual ghosts. The bed itself was still there, but it had been stripped. The floral duvet cover and matching crocheted afghan were gone. So were the pillows, decorative and other-wise. The dresser—which had held a jewellery box, a lamp, and a noisy old clock—was empty, and all the drawers hung open. The attached mirror was cracked, flinging our broken appearances back at us. My gaze drifted to the pinkish swath of skin on my jaw and lingered there for a moment. A few more days, and I probably wouldn't be able to tell that anything had happened.

I wasn't sure how I felt about that.

The closet was open, and it looked like there had been some sort of explosion within. Clothes had burst outward, leaving sad garments strewn all over the floor. Grandpa's button-down shirts, polos, and khakis lay like victims of a bombing. Annoyed, I reached down and grabbed his favourite striped polo.

"Assholes," I muttered as I grabbed a hanger and slipped the shirt back onto it. "If they didn't want old-people clothes, they could've just left them alone."

Click frowned at the shirt. I held it up against him, gauging the size.

"You want it? It might fit you."

He tilted his head, still staring at me. Finally, he looked down at the shirt, then pointed to it.

"It was my grandfather's. He won't be needing it."

He frowned.

"His name was Duncan."

Click just blinked at me. I sighed and hung the shirt up in the closet.

"Don't worry. You don't have to pronounce it. Come on." I edged past him and stepped back into the hall. I would deal with the rest of the clothing explosion later. After I had checked the rest of the house.

The bathroom looked like someone had used it at some point, judging by the mildewy towels crumpled on the floor. It didn't smell too great in there, either. The toilet lid was open, revealing the stained interior . . . but, thankfully, nothing else.

There were two more doors in the cramped hallway. One led to the smaller bedroom that Grandpa had used as his office. The large metal desk was still there. The chair was gone, though. The two short file cabinets that flanked the desk were closed. Grandpa had always kept them locked, so that wasn't surprising. What was surprising was that nobody had tried to pry them open. There were no scratches on the drawers at all. Then again, who would've wanted some old man's tax receipts?

I turned to the final door, which was closed. Click reached out and laid his hand on it, almost as if he was feeling for heat. Buddy immediately scratched at the door.

"Lee-ah."

"Yeah. This is my room. *Was* my room." I sighed and grasped the doorknob. "I don't even know if I want to look."

Click gently grasped my wrist, as if to pull my hand away from the knob. I shook my head.

"It's okay. It's just . . . it's probably going to be hard to see."

He didn't try to stop me again, so I took a deep breath and twisted the doorknob. The door swung into the room with a squeak of hinges. I let out a huff of air.

It was almost disappointing. Maybe I was hoping that the room would be totally trashed, and I'd have an excuse to feel some sort of righteous anger. But the place didn't look much different than when I'd left it. Aside from the stripped bed (seriously, what was with the linen bandits in this part of town?), all the furniture was still there. My ergonomic stool sat under the desk. *Probably because the kids who broke in here couldn't figure out what it was,* I thought, a wry smile twisting my lips. The corkboard above the desk still had all its pushpins, though they weren't holding anything up. (I'd taken everything down before leaving.) The curtains hung limp and dusty on either side of the window. On the far side of the room, the closet doors stood open, revealing all the empty hangers still lined up on the rod. Whoever had ransacked the house must've liked my style more than Grandpa's, because there was nothing left.

Buddy jumped up on the bed and put his paws on the windowsill, trying to see out into the backyard. He wasn't quite tall enough. Click and I could see out, though. I leaned closer to him and pointed so he could follow my finger.

"See that gap between the house and the evergreen? You can see the east wing of the high school."

Click said nothing for a moment. Then he turned to me. "Ree-fah."

"No. That's to the west." I jerked my thumb over to the left. "My bedroom window faces north." I looked down at Buddy, who had given up trying to see out and looked like he was about to settle himself on the bare mattress for a nap. My first instinct was to tell him to get down. Realistically, though, there had probably been worse things on that mattress in the last two years than a dog.

I went to the desk and pulled open the top drawer. To my surprise, the drawer organizer was still there, along with a few pens and pencils. Beneath that was a yellow legal pad, seemingly untouched. I wasn't sure what that said about the residents of Kenyonville. Didn't anyone ever need to write a note? Was nobody keeping any sort of journal? Maybe they had, at first. Back when we'd all had hope of the nightmare ending. What was the point of keeping a record, though, if nobody would ever get to read it?

I slipped my hand into the drawer and felt up under the top of the desk. There was a little lip that I'd found when I was a kid, just large enough to hold tiny treasures . . . like the crystal figurine I'd stolen from one of the boutiques in town when I was seven. Grandma had found it in the drawer while she was cleaning my room. I wasn't sure how. Maybe she'd bumped the desk and the trinket had fallen into the drawer. In any case, I hadn't used that hiding place for another decade. I just hoped what I'd stashed there hadn't fallen and been swiped.

It took a few seconds of breathless fumbling before my fingertips finally snagged what I was looking for. I pulled the cord out of the drawer, expelling a breath of relief as I did so, and held it up triumphantly. Click just frowned at it.

"This," I said, swinging it a little, watching the wooden ball on the end sway back and forth like a hypnotist's pendulum, "means that things are about to get a *lot* more comfortable."

He still looked confused, but I didn't feel like trying to explain. Instead, I grabbed my desk stool and pulled it out the door into the hallway, positioning it under the hatch in the ceiling. Pressing one hand to the wall for balance in the dimly lit space, I climbed up.

"I didn't want anyone getting up here," I explained as I slipped the cord through the metal loop on the hatch. "There's no food, but . . ." I shook my head and climbed down before moving the stool out of the way. Then I grabbed the bead on the end of the cord and pulled. The hatch opened up with a groan of resistance, and I stepped back as the mechanism slid the wooden ladder down in front of me. I glanced at Click, then waved my hand. "Come on. Let's see what's salvageable."

The attic was dusty and felt slightly damp. I wasn't sure if there was a leak in the roof somewhere, or if it was just the ambient air from all the recent rain. The windows let in just enough light that I could see the attic hadn't been touched. In fact, when I crawled onto the plywood floor, my knees left trails through the dust. I got out of the way so Click could follow me up, then sat back on my heels as I brushed the dust from my hands.

The plastic bins with our winter clothes were stacked in the corner on the far side of the north-facing window. For once in my life, I was thankful that the closets in the house were so small that we'd had to swap out our clothes with the seasons. Along the west wall were boxes of Christmas decorations, including a long cardboard one that held the artificial tree. By the south window sat stacks of papers, magazines, and books: the photos and drawings and printed-out pictures from my disassembled vision board; my collection of young adult novels (mostly dystopian and post-apocalyptic stories . . . concepts that seemed darkly funny now); Grandma's old gardening magazines with the dirt-stained pages. But it was the stack of shiny plastic zipper bags in the southeast corner of the attic that really got me excited. I stood up, keeping to a crouch so I wouldn't hit my head on the sloped ceiling, and shuffled over to check things out.

"Yes," I whispered as I pulled the top bag off the stack. It was my winter quilt, the one Grandma had made for me for my thirteenth birthday. I hadn't exactly been thrilled at the time (I'd wanted a new phone), but now all I could feel was the gratitude rushing through my veins like a warm cup of tea. *Thank you, Grandma*, I thought, feeling tears prick at my eyes as I unzipped the bag. The quilt smelled a bit stale, but that was nothing a quick trip through the washer and dryer wouldn't fix. The heavy quilt for Grandpa's bed was there, too, along with the set of throw pillows that matched. Since all the actual pillows in the house seemed to have been pilfered, they would have to do. Given how much time I'd spent in the last couple of years without a pillow at all, though . . . I wasn't about to turn up my nose at the frilly things.

I grabbed the bags with the quilts and handed them to Click, then took the pillows myself. As I glanced out the window, I noticed the dimming of the light. It wasn't a very bright day to begin with, but I could tell that the afternoon was wearing on.

"Let's get the quilts washed. Then we can make the beds."

Click's eyebrows rose. I shook my head.

"I'm not sharing with Buddy. He smells."

"Vee-kah," he said, letting go of the armful of quilts with one hand to tap his nose. My throat got so tight that I was afraid I was going to choke. I turned back to the window.

"I don't think . . . I don't think we should talk about him. Not yet."

Click was silent, as usual. When I finally dared to look at him, he was watching me with a perplexed frown. I waved my hand, indicating the ladder.

"Go on. Climb down. I'll start the laundry, and then we can put the food away while we're waiting. Sound good?"

He gave me a thumbs up, but he looked pretty unsure. It was hard to tell whether he didn't understand me or if he just didn't know why we couldn't talk about . . . certain people. I didn't feel like pursuing the matter, though, and to my great relief, he didn't seem to, either. He just grasped the bagged quilts with one arm and descended the ladder slowly, leaving me to try to compose myself in the dusty attic.

CHAPTER 3

THE CHAIR

While the washing machine was humming and sloshing in the basement, Click and I stood in the kitchen and went through the backpack that C-Roy had insisted we take. Frankly, I hadn't wanted anything from him; he'd done more than enough. But I did have another human and a dog to think about. I didn't want either of them starving under my watch.

The weight of the bag was explained by the five cans at the bottom. I lined them up on the counter, my mouth watering at the thought of cracking them open and eating what was inside: two cans of kidney beans, one can of chickpeas, one can of baby beets, and one can of sausages (which made me do a double take). There were also some foil packets of cheese-sauce powder that looked promising. A box of sugary cereal took up quite a bit of volume in the bag, but I couldn't really be that annoyed; it looked like a fun treat. There were two rolls of tablets that were labelled as some sort of watermelon-flavoured electrolyte drink. And, finally, the real treasure: a hefty plastic bag full of trail mix.

"Jackpot," I mumbled, turning the packet over to see what was inside. I saw a variety of nuts, as well as chocolate chips, pretzel bits . . . and raisins. I set the bag down on the counter and turned back to the backpack. C-Roy had added a few more items. I pulled them out, one at a time, and arranged them with the rest of the stash: a bottle of shampoo, a bar of glycerin soap, and what looked like half a packet of maxi pads . . . which would've been much appreciated had I actually needed them. But my body was obviously still in survival mode, since I hadn't had a visit from Aunt Flo in many months. Folded and tucked into an interior pocket was what I thought were just a few blank pieces of paper . . . until I pulled them out and smoothed them open on the counter. "Huh."

Click pointed to the word scrawled across the top of the page.

"September," I told him. Shaking my head slowly, I flipped the top page over, revealing a similar page with another grid of hand-drawn, numbered boxes. "October. November. December." I quickly flipped through the rest. There were twelve sheets, taking us all the way to the next August. "It's a calendar." I flipped back to September, noticing that someone had drawn a little star in the box for the second day of the month. It was the first time I'd known the actual date in a long time, and I couldn't help but be somewhat grateful to C-Roy for taking the time to make this for us. But hot on the heels of that feeling was more throat-clenching misery as another memory tried to weasel its way into my head. For a moment, all I could think about was an imaginary planner with pink kittens on it. Clearing the misery from my throat, I turned away and set the calendar down against the wall under the outlet for the old landline. Then I pulled open the drawer underneath.

Grandpa had always called it "The Black Hole," but it was just a junk drawer. And it was still pretty full. I rummaged around—moving aside leaky batteries with crusty ends, pencils with broken points, and half-used pads of sticky notes—until I came across what I was looking for. I pulled out the stack of bright pink tags we'd been given by the evacuation team and tore one off the top. Leaving Click with a puzzled expression, I hurried to the front door. It was still unlatched, so I simply pulled it open and found the nail that had been hammered into the wooden doorframe outside. Carefully, I slipped the plus-shaped slit over the nail and pressed the ticket against the hard surface. I wasn't sure if it would make any difference (or if it would make things a whole lot worse for us at some point), but the last thing I wanted was someone just barging in to what they thought was an unoccupied house.

I closed the door as quietly as I could, careful to make sure it latched this time, then turned the deadbolt. The next thing I heard was a thump from upstairs, and then Buddy appeared, hopping down the steps with his little legs. When he reached the bottom, he shook himself out again, stared up at me for a moment, sneezed, and trotted into the kitchen. With a sigh, I followed him.

"What ever happened to Katja?" I asked, watching as Click bent down to scoop Buddy into his arms. I wasn't sure what he was doing as he made his way over to the sink. "Click?"

He pointed to the tap, then to the dog.

"Put him down. I'll find a bowl or something."

He did as I asked while I went in search of something suitable. Most of the dishes were gone. They weren't lying broken on the floor, so I assumed they'd been taken to be used. Given that many people had left behind most of their stuff (including dishes) during the evacuation, I wasn't sure why anyone needed *our* dishes. Unless someone had had a plate-breaking party and wanted to replenish their cupboards.

There were a couple of cereal bowls left, along with one small plate that was tucked at the back, seemingly overlooked. But I figured we'd want to use those for ourselves. So I kept looking and eventually found Grandma's old stash of used cream-cheese containers. I got one out, rinsed it in the sink (it was a bit dusty, just like everything else), and filled it with water before setting it on the floor for Buddy. He started lapping at it right away, the noise loud in the quiet room. I watched for a few seconds, then shook my head.

"He's going to need to pee."

Click gave me a thumbs up.

"Just don't let him pee in the house. Okay?" The sound was making me thirsty, so I checked the cupboard with the glasses. For some reason, all the everyday ones were gone, but the wineglasses were still there. I pulled down a couple, smiling wryly. "Guess we're getting fancy."

After pouring our drinks, I opened the bag of trail mix and separated out two small piles. Click plucked out a few raisins and crouched down, hand outstretched. I quickly grabbed his wrist and hauled him back up. He frowned, looking perplexed.

"Dogs can't eat raisins. Or chocolate chips. Or macadamia nuts." I peered at the mixture of snacks on the counter. "I don't think there are macadamias in there. Still. That's pretty much a doggie doom snack."

"Bah-dee," Click said, patting his stomach with his free hand.

"I know. But you can't feed him trail mix." I reached for the can of sausages and grabbed the pull-tab on top. "He can have one of these."

The sausages smelled disgusting. Well, they smelled disgusting to me. But Buddy turned his nose upward, trying to sniff while he licked the water from his scruffy beard. I held the open can toward Click, who abandoned the raisins and plucked out a sausage. The greyish thing looked like a turd. Or a disembodied finger. I shuddered. But Buddy gobbled it up, then licked Click's fingers for good measure.

"I guess these belong to the dog," I said, lifting the can and turning it around to try to see an expiration date. "We'll keep these in the fridge. He can have one a day for now. Until we find more food."

Click gave me a thumbs up, stared at his thumb, and then licked it.

"Tasty?"

His nose wrinkled a little. I couldn't help letting out a grunt of laughter.

I spent the next few minutes putting the sausages in the fridge (which was, thankfully, still working . . . and empty) and everything else into the pantry cupboard. Click picked at the trail mix, trying each nut and fruit separately with a contemplative expression that made me think of some sort of wine snob. I just gathered my portion of mix into my hand and shoved it into my mouth. As soon as the food hit my stomach, I felt really sleepy. I would've liked to sit down, but there were no stools like in Niesha's old kitchen, and the small table and chairs that had stood by the window were missing. I wondered about that for a moment, but decided I was too tired to really care. There was always the dining room. Well, as long as *that* furniture was still there.

"I'm going to go put the quilt in the dryer," I said. Click raised his eyebrows. "Never mind." I headed for the basement steps. "Take Buddy to pee. Out front," I clarified when I saw him glance at the back door. He gave me a thumbs up, so I knew he understood. Then I made my way back down into the spidery basement.

—

It was still technically summer, and we had our jackets, so I didn't worry too much about the fact that only one of the quilts was ready by bedtime. I spread it out over the mattress in Grandpa's room, then got Click and Buddy settled. The dog was *really* gassy after that sausage, and I didn't want to listen to complaints from his back end all night, so I said goodnight to Click and headed for my room. It felt a bit weird crashing on the bare mattress with nothing but a throw pillow for comfort. But that didn't stop me from falling asleep almost immediately.

I awoke, surprised, in the early dawn light. It had been ages since I'd slept so well. Even at C-Roy's— under the protection of one of the most respected bosses in town—my sleep had been fitful. I rolled onto my back, stretching my toes in one direction and my arms in the other. I could smell my armpits when I did that. *Shower day,* I thought as I hauled myself out of bed and tiptoed to the hallway.

It was dark, even with the two bedroom doors

open, so I ran my fingers against the wall as I made my way to the bathroom. My reflection in the mirror was just a shadowy blob. I splashed some water on my face, more to wake myself up than anything else, then had a quick pee. My stomach, appearing to wake up and notice that it was hungry, complained loudly. I slapped my hand over it. Like that was going to help.

I tiptoed down the stairs in my bare feet, feeling a little nervous about leaving my shoes up in my room, just in case I had to make a run for it. *You need to change that mindset*, I thought. *This is your life now. You can make it as normal as possible, or you can live in fear forever.* I wasn't sure I *could* live in fear forever. It was tiring. I supposed that only left me one option.

And that was how I ended up standing in the doorway to the living room, staring at the back of Grandpa's recliner while my heart pounded so hard I was afraid Buddy would hear it from upstairs.

It's just an ugly chair. An inanimate object. It can't hurt you.

My mind wanted to argue back against itself. I clenched my fists—which were, surprisingly, not glowing—and took a step forward, edging to the left of the chair. I took another step. The bare floor under my feet felt dusty. *Maybe I should sweep first. I mean, the chair's not going anywhere, right?*

"No," I whispered. "Just do it. Get it over with."

The third step took me level with the arm of the recliner. I kept my gaze fixed straight ahead on the loveseat at the far side of the room. One of the seat cushions was missing. I glared at the empty space, realizing that I hadn't blinked in an awfully long time.

I kept walking until I'd passed the chair. Then I stopped. The fireplace gaped to my left. To my right, Grandpa's old TV, a pitifully small flatscreen, sat on its console table. A flash of indignation swept through me, followed almost immediately by dark amusement. *Well, at least we still have a TV . . . if only because people thought it was too crappy to steal.*

I knew I was stalling, but I just couldn't bring myself to turn around. I knew what I was going to see. Realistically, it probably wasn't going to be as bad as I remembered. It had been years. These things . . . faded.

At least, I hoped they did.

Closing my eyes, I took a deep breath and turned around. My heart pounded in my ears for a few seconds before I let the breath out in a rush. As I did, I heard another sort of pounding noise, this time coming from the stairs. I opened my eyes to find Click stepping into the doorway of the living room.

"I . . ." I began. But the words stuck in my throat. Before I could stop it, my gaze drifted to the recliner. I jerked, almost in anticipation of being startled. But I wasn't. Not really. What I saw was exactly what I'd expected.

Click padded into the room and came to stand next to me. I could hear Buddy in the hallway, his nails clicking as he explored. But he didn't come to us, which left the room feeling even emptier as the two of us stood there, staring at the chair. Click probably had no idea what we were even looking at. But he didn't try to ask.

I slipped my hand into my jacket pocket. Tucked in there with the exit pass from Dr. Frazier (which I was still carrying around, even though it was completely useless within the Zone itself) was the folded photo I'd salvaged from its broken frame a few months earlier. I opened it up and angled it toward Click. He took it, almost reverently, and gave it a careful examination.

"Lee-ah?" he said at last, pointing to the girl in the middle of the photo. I'd changed in the seven years or so since it had been taken, but obviously not past the point of recognizability. I nodded.

"Yeah. And those are my grandparents: Duncan and Tasha."

Click tilted his head a little, then turned to look at me. He looked back at the photo again.

"My dad was Asian. I'm not sure what kind of Asian, though. Probably Chinese or Korean. He didn't stick around long enough for my grandparents to find out much about him. And then my mom took off, so I guess I'll never know exactly why I'm not blond like the rest of the family. Not without doing a DNA test."

Click returned the photo to me. I contemplated setting it on the mantel where I could look at it, but decided that I probably wasn't going to be spending much time in that room. So I folded the photo and slipped it back into my pocket. Click suddenly pointed at the chair. I jerked as if he'd slapped me.

"What?"

"Dah-kah."

"Duncan?"

He gave me a thumbs up. I turned back to the chair. The stain was so much more visible now, even as my eyes filled with tears and my throat filled with what felt like sand. I coughed and shook my head.

"Someone killed him."

Click stepped closer to me and wrapped his arms around my body. For some reason, that made me want to both laugh and cry. I resigned myself to a small grunt.

"It was a year after the Rift opened up. Food was getting scarce. People were just starting to make alliances. And Grandpa..." I took a deep, shaky breath to try to steady my nerves. "He didn't trust the Rifters in this part of town. He was right not to. But I didn't think... I didn't think they would do what they did."

Click's arms were steady as he held me, waiting for me to go on. The pain I'd carried for the last two-and-a-half years was so heavy. It was too heavy. I couldn't carry it by myself anymore.

"Permanent Marc had just taken control. His goons were out looking for pledges of loyalty, making threats to people who wouldn't accept. Grandpa told them—politely—to fuck off. We thought that was the end of it. And then, a few days later, I came back from one of the checkpoints and found him dead." My throat tightened with a squeak. "Someone had shot him in the head. Right through the back of the chair. They just left him like that. And I didn't even get any food that day. If I'd been here..."

For only the second time in recent memory, I felt the tears start to flow again. I tried to reach up to wipe them away, but Click had my arms pinned.

"Viktor knew," I said, knowing I was probably going to regret speaking his name, but doing it anyway. "He knew there was something I wasn't telling him. I don't know *why* I didn't tell him. Maybe I thought he'd make a stupid joke or something. But ... I know he wouldn't have. He wasn't—" My voice caught. All I could think about at that moment was what would've happened if I *had* told him. I would've found myself in his arms, cradled in shared pain the way I was at that moment with Click. "He probably thought I didn't trust him," I said with a sob. "But I did. I would've trusted him with my life. It was myself that I didn't trust."

"Lee-ah."

I blinked away the tears, still staring at the recliner. At the small, brownish stain I'd found behind Grandpa's head when I'd returned home and discovered him, eerily still, in his favourite chair. "I miss him so much," I whispered, not bothering to qualify the statement.

Click let go and stepped in front of me. I dashed

the tears from my cheeks, watching as his golden eyes searched my features. He reached up and laid his fingertips on my forehead, so gently that I barely felt them. "Vee-kah," he said softly, punctuating the name with the familiar clicking sound.

"No. I don't . . . I can't."

"Vee-kah." He gently tapped his fingers against my skin, the touch like a hummingbird's wings.

"He's gone."

His fingers continued to tap.

"Click, I *can't*." I closed my eyes. *I don't want to think about him. If I do . . .* The tears started again. "I know he was in pain. But I thought he was . . . I didn't think he would . . ." A surge of anger shot through me, startling me so much that I opened my eyes. "How could he *do* that?" I asked, my voice nearly a shout. "He threw away *everything* when he stepped in front of that truck. And now—"

"Vee-kah," Click repeated. I took a step back, forcing him to pull his hand away. But he just transferred it to his own forehead.

"Maybe I don't want to remember him!" I shouted. "Maybe it just hurts too fucking much!" My hands were flaring, casting a weird glow around the shadowy living room. Click took a quick step to the side, almost as if he knew what I was about to do. The two Riftballs splattered on the chair, obliterating the bloodstain for a moment, but leaving the fabric frustratingly untouched. Letting out a wordless scream, I hurled another ball. And another. And another. And I only stopped when I saw Buddy in the foyer, coming to see what was going on, because I didn't want to hurt him. Nobody else needed to get hurt. Too many people had already been hurt. "Fuck him!" I shouted, the words distorted by sobs. "I loved the stupid asshole. I loved him." Shaking the remaining Rift energy from my fingers, I blinked away the tears. Click stepped in front of me again, gazing steadily into my eyes. "Doesn't it hurt?" I asked.

He blinked, his eyebrows twitching into a frown. It almost looked like he was listening. At last, he reached out, took my hand, and placed it on my own chest.

"I know he's still in my heart," I said. "But it's not enough. I want him here. With us. I want him back. The only reason I sent him away was because I thought I was helping him." Swallowing was painful. I tried again. It felt like there was a fist-sized rock in my throat. "He must've felt so abandoned. I promised him I wouldn't leave him . . . and then I made him leave the Zone. He probably died hating me—"

"Lee-ah." Click's voice was a gentle scolding. I looked down at our hands. And then I closed my eyes.

I didn't know how Click was doing it. How he could be so . . . *okay*. Especially after what had happened. I knew he cared. I knew he'd loved Viktor, too. Maybe it was a cultural thing. Maybe people in Reefa (wherever the hell that was) grieved differently. I had no idea about their beliefs or their religion. I didn't even know if they practiced a religion.

But I wanted to be able to deal with this the way he was. Calmly. Lovingly. Maybe he was right. If I just let those thoughts in . . . If I just let *Viktor* in . . .

I miss you, I thought, keeping my eyes closed as I felt our hands rise and fall with each of my breaths. *You were the best friend I had in this hellhole. Maybe, if things had been different . . .* My cheeks started to feel warm. I opened my eyes to find Click staring at me, a tiny little smile on his face. I let my hand fall.

"What?" I demanded. But he didn't have time to answer before I noticed Buddy, who had seemingly finished his exploration of the living room. He was sitting on the chair. *The* chair. "Get down!"

The dog jumped down, skittering on the floor. Click turned, frowning, and regarded the recliner for a moment. He glanced at me, then turned back to the chair. The next thing I knew, he was pushing it toward the front door. I didn't bother to argue. Instead, I joined him, and, together, we dragged the awful memory down to the curb and left the stained piece of furniture in the shade of an overgrown maple tree.

When I stepped back into the house a few moments later, I felt like I could breathe again.

CHAPTER 4

THE AWFUL WHY

It was surprising how much there was to do in the post-apocalyptic remains of a small town. At least in a mostly intact house, anyway.

I got the winter clothes out of the attic and readied them for us to wear. I even managed to get Click out of his clothes long enough to wash the denim jacket and jeans, though he was adamant that his beaded shirt and weird skirt were not to be trifled with. I didn't really argue, since I didn't know what would happen when they went through the washing machine, and I didn't want to be responsible for destroying his sense of security. I'd had a favourite sweater when I was a kid . . . and I'd been devastated when Grandma had overlooked an open metal zipper on one of my pairs of jeans, resulting in the sweater developing a few holes.

The vacuum was gone, but the broom and dustpan

were still there, so I swept every corner of the house. Click seemed to want to help, so I stuck a pair of fluffy socks on his hands and sent him off to dust every flat surface he could reach. He got the idea right away, and it kept him busy for hours. Buddy followed him at first, but then got bored and curled up on the loveseat in the living room, getting white hair all over the remaining cushion. (The loss of the vacuum was deeply felt.)

I got the books out of the attic and brought them downstairs, filling up the built-in bookcases on either side of the fireplace. The TV was useless without a signal, and there was no DVD player, so the small screen remained in the room like a decorative piece. I didn't really mind. There was plenty of reading material.

The food situation was a little trickier. We made C-Roy's gifts last as long as we could, but I could only stretch trail mix and canned beets so far. Technically, we were in Permanent Marc's territory, but I had no idea what the protocols were or how anyone was getting fed in that part of town. Joshua's turf, however, was right across the street, and I knew how things operated there: not very well. The cache houses weren't always well guarded, and they were spread so thin that it would've been next to impossible to keep track of inventory.

Which was good for us.

On our first raid, we came home with two cans of

kidney beans, half a bag of Cheeznudles, and a can of dog food . . . which Click insisted on trying, even though it smelled like something that had crawled out of a ditch and died. We also came back with some pretty good prospects for future raids. Spaced out, of course, if we didn't want Joshua's goons getting wise to the thefts.

Since we were ripping off Joshua, Buddy stayed at home for his own safety. But when Click and I returned after one of our runs to find tooth marks in the legs of the dining room table, we knew we needed a dog-sitter. It wasn't like we ever found a huge haul that was too big for one person to carry, and Click didn't have Rifthands, anyway . . . so I made him stay behind with the dog while I went out to find food. The arrangement seemed to work just fine, even if it was a little lonely for me. But without any other people (or dogs) to worry about, I could work faster, getting in and out and back home within a couple of hours. And it was kind of nice to be greeted by a dog when I returned.

It was always nice to feel wanted.

Had I known I would be returning to our house one day, I might have chosen not to use the vegetable garden as a burial ground. What was done was done, though. The yard was still spacious and fairly private, so, one day a few weeks after we'd moved in, I decided to tackle it. I didn't have any seeds (and most of what *had* been growing in the gardens appeared to have been pilfered long ago), but the yard was a mess, and I could almost hear Grandma's disappointed voice in my ear.

"Keep Buddy inside," I told Click as I stepped out onto the back porch. From behind me, I heard a whine. It was as if the dog had understood me.

The detached garage looked untouched, which was pretty amazing. That meant Grandpa's pickup truck was most likely still inside. So were Grandma's gardening tools. I turned to Click, who was hovering in the open doorway. Buddy sat beside him, staring out into the yard, calmly sniffing the air.

"You don't know how to pick a lock, do you?"

Click blinked, then looked at the garage. But I didn't get an actual answer, so I just walked over there, my legs whispering through the knee-high grasses. The small door on the side was locked, as I'd expected. With a sigh, I went through the gate to try the larger, articulated door on the front. When it actually moved a few inches, I dropped it in surprise. It landed with a thump that brought Click running.

"Don't get too excited," I said as I bent down to get a better grasp on the handle. "Everything's probably gone."

But when we lifted the heavy door, everything *wasn't* gone. Grandpa's truck was still there, albeit dusty. The doors were locked, but nobody had smashed the windows to try to force their way in. There was no graffiti, either . . . which suggested this was the first time the garage had been opened in a while.

"Holy shit," I whispered as chaotic thoughts started to tumble through my head. Silly thoughts, really. Vehicles weren't practical anymore. And an operational truck in the Rift Zone would attract *way* too much attention. Which sucked, because all I wanted to do was drive down to C-Roy's part of town and get some more provisions.

Click trailed his fingers over the grimy windows, seemingly transfixed by the vehicle. I shook my head.

"Sorry. No Sunday drives."

He turned to me, looking confused.

"It's been sitting here for a couple of years. It probably won't even start. And driving it through town would be dangerous. We'd make ourselves a huge target."

He pulled his fingers away from the glass. "Vee-kah," he said.

I just stared at him for a moment as a hot spike of anger shot through my body. "Seriously? Don't remind me."

With a frown, he pointed northwest. Toward the checkpoint. I snorted.

"You want to blast through the checkpoint in this? That's a great way to get shot." I shook my head. "Besides, there's nothing for us out there now. He's gone. Dead. He's been dead for weeks. We might as well stay here."

Click looked so troubled that I wished I hadn't said anything at all. I wasn't sure what he was talking about. I wasn't sure if he even understood *me* half the time. Viktor had claimed that Click understood English, but I had my doubts. Wouldn't he speak more of it if that were the case?

I turned away from the truck and headed for the shelves at the back of the garage. Grandma's gardening supplies were still there, so I grabbed her old gloves, the bucket with her hand tools, and her pink plastic watering can.

"Come on. You can help me weed around Lord Hulkington."

—

Working in the yard became my new favourite thing to do. It wasn't really gardening—the gardens were beyond help at that point—but there was something soothing about trimming Lord Hulkington, snipping at the grass with a pair of garden shears (the lawnmower and jerrycans were missing, so somebody had been in the garage after all), and watering the few plants that had managed to survive the years of neglect. Click and Buddy mostly amused themselves. Sometimes Click helped me, even though I didn't need him to and rarely asked. Most of the time, though, they just played together. Buddy liked fetch, and there were plenty of sticks for that. He also liked to make Click chase him around the yard. Hide and seek was another favourite, although Buddy seemed to find his human friend suspiciously quickly. I listened as they played, wondering if Click was making some sort of noise that only dogs could hear. But I never did hear anything. Maybe Buddy was just using his nose.

While they played, I let myself sink into a sort of meditation, allowing thoughts of a certain person to step back into my mind. At first, I didn't let that go on for too long. But, for some weird reason, I started to feel worse if I cut those little reveries off too soon ... so I just let them come and let his voice lead the conversation wherever it wanted to go.

"You *could* deal with this overgrown lawn really fast," he said one day as I crouched in the back corner by the fence, chewing away at the grass with a pair of shears that were growing duller by the day. I closed my eyes for a moment, a little smile playing on my lips, as I imagined him kneeling next to me, blowing a raspberry and letting his hand flare.

"Do you want to burn down the whole neighbourhood?"

"I wouldn't. Only living stuff is affected." He turned and looked back at the house. "That doesn't look like a living thing to me."

"Sure it is. A home is a living thing."

"Only metaphorically. Or maybe if you've got a good mould colony growing in the shower grout."

"Gross."

He shook off the pink and tilted forward, leaning his hands on the grass and fixing me with a smile. I felt my own lips twitch in response. In those daydreams, he looked the way he had the day I'd met him: tall, dark, and handsome (as long as you were looking at his right side). Rasputin had never happened. Dr. Bryan hadn't done the surgery. I could still see the twinkle in that beautiful, dark eye.

"I knew it," he said.

"What?"

"You had a thing for me."

"Shut up."

He laughed. I closed the shears and set them down on the grass, still keeping my eyes shut. The dream me reached out and brushed the backs of my fingers over his scar.

"I miss you," I said quietly.

"I know. I miss you, too, Léa."

"I'm sorry I broke my promise."

He nodded, reaching up to fold his fingers around my hand. "You were only trying to help me." Pulling my hand away from his cheek, he fixed me with a gentle look. "I would've broken the same promise."

"You would've abandoned your blind best friend?"

He kissed the back of my hand. "You didn't abandon me."

"Then why'd you feel the need to jump in front of a truck?"

He froze. It didn't look natural. I shook my head,

trying to jumpstart the daydream, but it was like a video that had stalled midstream. I opened my eyes with a sigh. The shears sat in front of me on the grass, which was wafting its clean, green scent toward my nose. Glancing around, I spotted Click standing a few feet away, Buddy's stick in hand. Instead of playing, he was watching me, a little smile on his face.

"Vee-kah," he said. I turned away, grabbing the shears.

"Whatever." I resumed my attack on the over-grown grass, feeling both annoyed and confused by my own reverie. Maybe, one day, I would be able to put an answer on Viktor's lips about the awful *why*.

CHAPTER 5

PERMITS

The next couple of months passed in a blur as Click and I settled in and built the best life we could.

I kept track of the passing days with the makeshift calendar, crossing off each square with a red marker I'd found in the junk drawer. It was old and dry, and even when I licked the tip, I could still only make faint pink marks . . . but, somehow, that colour seemed fitting, given where we were.

It was mid-November—November fourteenth, to be exact—when there was a knock on the front door. Click and I were sitting at the table in the dining room (as we always did), eating a meagre meal of bean and Cheeznudle casserole. Technically, it was my twenty-first birthday, and for the briefest of moments, I had the thought that someone was coming to celebrate the milestone. But that ridiculous notion didn't last long, and my stomach clenched painfully around its miserable birthday dinner. Click and I just stared at each other across the table. Buddy—sitting in his usual spot in the open doorway so he could stare hungrily at us while we ate—reacted first, standing up and turning to face the front of the house. Back when he'd been called Lex and lived with his former owner, he'd been a real yapper. Now, it was almost like he'd forgotten what he was supposed to do when someone intruded upon his territory. He let out a little whuff, his tail giving an uncertain wag.

I turned back to Click, holding my finger to my lips. It wasn't like he was going to yell out, "Who's there?" But, still. My heart hammered in my ears as I very carefully set my fork down on the table, trying to make as little noise as possible. *Maybe, if we don't answer, they'll go away,* I thought . . . only to have that hope dashed a moment later as the knock came again. For a moment, I regretted putting up that pink ticket. But, if I hadn't, whoever it was might not have bothered to knock. The last thing I wanted to worry about was people just barging in.

The problem was that, with the ticket, we were announcing our presence. Someone knew we were here. Even if we didn't answer the door now, we were probably going to have to answer it sometime. When they came back. And if we never answered . . . well, someone might assume the house had been abandoned. Or someone had died. After all, Buddy's owner's house had had an occupancy ticket on the door.

When the third knock came, I stood up and tiptoed to the foyer. There was no peephole in the door, and the curtains on the flanking windows were almost opaque, so there was no way for me to discreetly see who was standing on the other side. It could've been anyone. Joshua's runners were at the top of the list, given that we were just a few steps from his turf. But Permanent Marc's people were also a distinct possibility. The house was technically in his territory. Just because we'd avoided a friendly neighbourhood meet-and-greet so far didn't mean we were never going to have to deal with the . . . what? Homeowners' association? I honestly didn't know. Technically, the house was probably mine. Being a homeowner at twenty-one might've seemed like a pretty cool thing, had that home not been in the middle of the Rift Zone and in the territory of one of the scariest bosses in town.

There really was no way to get any answers about who was on the other side of the door, other than opening it. So I did . . . and found myself looking down at the scarred forehead of a young girl.

"Shit," I muttered. "How old are you?"

She frowned, and the two round scars pulled a little as she did so. *One of Permanent Marc's runners, then.* My skin itched just looking at those things. But there was something else that itched deep inside my brain. A memory. Or . . .

"You didn't get enough of my stuff the first time?" I asked as the familiarity finally slapped the memory forward. I could see the moment when the girl remembered, too. Her eyes widened a little, but she stood her ground, placing one hand on the doorframe and leaning forward. She was probably trying to look tough, but it was a bit laughable.

"Do you have a permit?" she asked.

I snorted. "Since when do I need a permit to live in my own house?"

"This isn't your house."

"Wanna bet?"

"Then why were you living at Ayla's a few months ago?"

"I was lonely."

She narrowed her eyes. "You're not lonely now?"

"Not really," I said. On cue, Buddy peeked around the corner of the door. The girl dropped her hand and took a step back, instantly disarmed.

"Oh! He's so cute!"

"Uh-huh." I tried to nudge Buddy back with my leg, but he knew a gushing teenager when he saw one, and he wanted to say hello. He stepped onto the porch, tail wagging, as the girl fell into a crouch. I took the opportunity to peek back around the door. Click was still sitting at the table. I waved my hand at him, so he slid off the chair and came to join me.

"I had a cat before," the girl said, her fingers massaging through the longer hair around Buddy's ears. "I always wanted a dog, but my mom didn't want to pick up the poop."

"But she'd clean a litter box?"

She shook her head. "There was no litter box. He was an outside cat." Glancing up, she spotted Click. One eyebrow rose. "What the hell are you wearing?"

"Are you seriously judging someone's appearance right now? Because you're not exactly one to—"

"This," she said, pointing at one of the scars, "is loyalty. Not fashion."

"Whatever."

Giving Buddy one last scratch, she stood up and let out an exasperated sigh. "Do you have a permit or not?"

"Where the fuck was I supposed to get a permit?"

"Where do you think?"

"If it's that important to him, he can come issue one himself." Even as the words were coming out of my mouth, my mind was screaming at me to stop talking. The girl smirked.

"Oh, I don't think you want him to do that. He doesn't appreciate squatters."

"Excuse me. This is *my* house. When your people killed the previous owner, it passed to me. If anyone is where they don't belong at this very moment, it's you."

Her eyes narrowed a little. It was amazing what a few months could do to a person. Before, this kid had been passive. A follower. Still worrying about what the older Rifters might do. Now, though, she was different. Harder, somehow. There might've been a few reasons for that. I was pretty sure they were all unpleasant.

"Where's Bennie?" I asked. Her eyes narrowed even more. *Bingo,* I thought.

"What's it to you?"

"Did she mouth off to the wrong Rifter?"

The girl's hand shot up at her side, glowing a brilliant pink. My heart jumped into my throat with such force that I almost coughed. A few months ago, my hands would've flared automatically. Now, though, it took a bit of effort for me to raise my own glowing hand.

"Seriously? You going to take me on?" Turning my palm downward, I wiggled my fingers and let the pink rain onto the porch, being careful not to catch Buddy in the shower. Then I drew the energy back and down, grounding it so fast that my hand looked like a flashlight that had just clicked off. The girl's eyes widened. "Yeah. I'm *really* good at controlling it."

"'Cause you're old."

"And you're still just a baby. Seriously. How old are you? Twelve?"

"Thirteen," she spat. "And I've had just as much experience with pinkhands as you."

"I doubt it."

Her mouth opened, then closed again. A twinge of triumph plucked at my pounding heart. I grabbed the edge of the door and started to push it closed.

"Bah-dee," Click sang softly. The dog looked up at the girl, then obediently jumped over the threshold and into the house.

"Send over the paperwork for the permit," I said, my heart pounding so hard and fast that I was surprised my voice didn't shake.

"He won't be happy about this."

"No shit. But I'm sure he has better things to do than waste time worrying about one little house on the border of his territory. We're minding our own business."

"Yeah, right." She slammed her non-glowing hand on the door, preventing me from closing it. "If we catch you stealing from—"

"We haven't been to any of your stupid caches. Joshua's got plenty of unguarded ones. Tell your boss."

"Why? We've got plenty of—"

"No," I said, cutting her off. "Tell him that so he knows we're not worth the trouble. We're not stealing from him. We're not interfering in any way. This was my home long before he ever took control. If he really has a problem with us living here, he can come talk to me, face to face."

She let out a humorous grunt of laughter. "He'd roast you in five seconds."

"He could try." I gave the door a shove, pushing her back. As soon as the door was closed, I threw the dead-bolt, making it clunk as loudly as I could so she'd get the message.

Buddy let out a whine and scratched at Click's leg. I shook my head slowly as I looked down at the dog.

"Hold it."

He turned to me and let out a soft huff. I walked back to the dining room and sat down at the table, even though my appetite was gone. Click took his place across from me. But he didn't start eating again, either. We just sat there, staring at each other, until I finally took a deep breath and let out a long sigh.

"I hope I didn't just sign our death warrant."

He blinked slowly, but his expression was impossible to read. A moment later, he picked up his fork—holding it awkwardly, like he always did—and resumed eating. I stared down at the orange-crusted beans, then closed my eyes.

"You're all right," Viktor said, sliding onto the chair to my left. He plucked a bean from my bowl and flicked it, sending it bouncing down the length of the table.

"Don't."

"I thought you hated Cheeznudles."

"I'll eat what I can get."

He leaned one elbow on the table and peered at me with his mismatched eyes. "She was just posturing, you know."

"What if she wasn't?"

"Then you'll deal with the donkeybutt if he comes knocking on the door."

"What if he just burns the whole place down with us inside?"

His eyebrows drew into a frown. "You really think Marc's that evil?"

"I have no idea anymore. I used to think people were generally okay. But now . . ."

"Niesha's okay. Click's okay. I'm okay. Right?"

"You really want me to answer that?"

He gasped dramatically and threw himself back in the chair. "You *mock* me."

"You make it easy."

With a grunt of amusement, he leaned a little closer. "You're just as powerful as all those donkey-butts, Léa. Remember that. Don't let them intimidate you. Don't be scared."

My throat tightened. "How can you say that? You lived here for three years, just like the rest of us."

"Most Rifters are just kids. I know you're probably not that familiar with the concept of real teenagers, being all sheltered and homeschooled—"

"Shut up."

He clamped his lips together. I shook my head.

"Sorry. I'm sorry. Don't stop talking to me."

"I won't," he said softly. "I'll be right here for as long as you need me. Okay?"

I nodded, but the tears were already starting. I opened my eyes to find a blurry Click staring at me, his fork poised over his nearly empty plate. Blinking, I grabbed my own fork and stabbed at the casserole while using my free hand to dash away the tears.

"Vee-kah," he said quietly. I swiped at my cheeks again, harder this time.

"Yeah. Fine. Grief takes time, okay?"

He gave me a tentative thumbs up before turning back to his plate. We finished our disgusting servings of casserole in silence.

CHAPTER 6

ALL THAT AND A BAG OF CHEEZNUDLES

It was getting cold. Early December didn't always mean snow in Kenyonville, but it didn't mean weather you wanted to get caught in, either. The rain was cold. The wind was cold. The air itself was cold, and my nose ended up streaming every time I went out on a run. Luckily, I was by myself, so I didn't have to worry about bad manners as I continually wiped the drips with the sleeve of my jacket.

I talked to Viktor in my head. Our relationship—at least, the imaginary one—grew stronger with each passing day. Sometimes, I imagined him holding my hand. There were times when I could almost feel it . . . but only for a few seconds. Then something—a distant shout, the call of a crow, the banging of an unlatched door in the wind—would snap me back to my lonely reality. I was getting better at it, though, able to hold on to him for longer and longer each time.

In the first week of December, I trudged down the street in the pouring rain, my hood pulled up, my arms wrapped around my middle. My canvas sneakers were soaked and my feet were freezing . . . even though I was wearing a pair of rather thick socks. Actually, my feet were freezing *because* I was wearing a pair of rather thick socks that were acting like sponges in the downpour. My body shivered violently. All I could think about was curling up on the couch with Click and Buddy, sipping a cup of hot electrolyte drink. Tea would've been nicer, but we didn't have that.

The cache house I'd decided on was deep in Joshua's territory, only a couple of blocks from his checkpoint. I stayed well away from that; Joshua might not have guarded his caches very well, but he did have his goons stationed around the checkpoint, making sure nobody got any handouts without proper authorization. *His* authorization. There was something about that setup that pissed me right off. It was like the kindergarteners being in charge of the college kids. But, in the Rift Zone, it had less to do with maturity and more to do with how far you were willing to go to maintain your power. People like Joshua? Well, we already knew he was willing to eat pets.

I turned and cut between a couple of houses, which soaked my jeans to my knees thanks to the unmowed grass. *Stupid rain*, I thought. *Stupid cache house. Stupid* far *cache house. Stupid far cache house that damn well better have something better than stupid Cheeznudles and marijuana after all this.*

My fingers were near frozen. I curled my hands into wet fists and stuffed them in my jacket pockets. I was getting the exit pass all wet. Not that it mattered. We'd blown that opportunity to live on the outside.

"You didn't have to follow me back in here," Viktor said, sort of startling me with his sudden presence. I ducked under a low-hanging branch, pushing the rain-beaded needles out of the way before letting the whole thing snap back in his face. "Hey! You trying to put out my good eye?"

"Are you seriously going to joke about that?"

"What else am I going to joke about?" He jogged a little ahead so he could turn around and walk backward through the overgrown grass. His jacket was soaked, and the raindrops were beading on his dark hair. Probably because it was so greasy.

"The Rift Zone is dead serious," I said.

"That's why I need to keep things light. You'll never survive if I don't."

I narrowed my eyes at him, but he just smiled and glanced over his shoulder.

"So . . . where are we going?"

"One of Joshua's caches."

"Cool. Maybe you'll find something good."

"Our definitions of 'good' are pretty different."

"Right. I forgot. You're a Cheezenudlephobe."

"You're a raisinphobe," I shot back. His eyebrows jumped, and he let out a short laugh.

"Um, that's normal, Léa. Those things are farting gross."

Shaking my head, I stumbled onto the sidewalk and turned to the right. He hurried to catch up.

"Are you cold? You look cold. You must be cold."

"No shit, Sherlock."

"The name's Viktor." He paused. "Actually, it's—"

"It's Viktor," I said quickly.

"I think I know my own name."

"You're Viktor," I said, my voice sounding so fierce that he backed away a step, holding up his hands.

"Okay."

"You're not who they say you are. You're not to blame for any of this."

"I did make you come back . . ."

"Huh. I don't remember you dragging me, kicking and screaming."

"I didn't give you much choice."

I sighed. "It was still my choice. What's out there for me?"

"Niesha's out there."

"Yeah, and she's got her own life and her own family. My family was here. Is here," I corrected myself.

"The Rift Zone isn't Click's home, either."

"It is for now. And probably forever."

He didn't say anything. He knew I was right. What

was supposed to be just a few weeks had turned into almost four years. Those fences and checkpoints were probably permanent.

We walked in silence until we reached the cache house. There was no pink ticket on the door. Joshua seemed to avoid using those things deep inside his territory. I had no idea why. Maybe he figured an occupancy ticket was some sort of challenge. And maybe it was, to someone like him. Still, he rarely had anyone guarding his caches. Safety with anonymity? But he obviously hadn't counted on runners from other territories figuring out where he kept all the best stuff.

"Well," Viktor said as we stood there, staring at the unadorned front door.

"If you're coming, you need to be quiet. I have to concentrate."

He pretended to zip his lips.

"You done?"

"Mmh-mmhm, mm-mmh."

"Shut up."

A grunt of amusement was all I got. Keeping my head down, I jogged up the front walk, trying to keep my footsteps light as I stepped onto the covered front porch. My jacket was shedding water like crazy, and I was leaving a very obvious sign of my presence. But, as I looked down, my stomach clenched a little.

"Looks like you're not the first person to hit this cache today," Viktor whispered. He stepped past me—and the wet spot on the porch—and peered through the window beside the door, but I doubted he could see much past the sheer curtain on the other side.

"Great."

"You'll have to get your Cheeznudles somewhere else."

"I don't want Cheeznudles."

"Condoms?"

I coughed and stared at the back of his head. He turned around, eyebrows high.

"What?"

"Who the hell would I be having sex with?"

He shrugged, then reached up to tighten his ponytail. I let out a snort.

"You?" I guessed.

"Why not?"

"Don't flatter yourself."

"You said you loved me."

"That doesn't mean I want to get started on the Rift Zone Repopulation Agenda with you."

His face brightened in an amused smile. "I see I'll have to explain a few things. Now, when a man and a woman want to make a baby, they probably *shouldn't* use a condom."

"Probably?"

"Accidents happen."

I shook my head. "I wouldn't need a condom to prevent getting knocked up by a ghost."

"A ghost?" His eyes widened, and he looked around. "Where?"

"Shut up," I said, and, even in my imagination, my voice was choked. I closed my eyes for a moment. This was the last thing I needed. Stepping into a cache house was not the best time to be distracted by an annoying echo from the past. I took a few deep breaths, listening to the raindrops drip from the eaves and even more droplets fall from my jacket onto the porch. There weren't any sounds coming from inside the house, though. When I opened my eyes and looked down, I saw that the wet spot from whoever else had been there wasn't that bad. In fact, it might've been a few hours old.

I tried the door, not surprised at all when it opened easily. Door locks were rarely used in Kenyonville anymore. Probably the only reason Viktor and Click had used them was because there was another way into their house. Trying to keep my jacket from rustling too much, I pushed the door open a little more and stepped inside. There was a doormat under my feet, which was a good thing; leaving wet footprints across the hardwood didn't seem like a smart move.

The kitchen was the most logical place to keep food . . . which meant that Joshua *never* kept it there. I could see that the kitchen was a mess, anyway. All the cupboard doors hung open, showing off the empty spaces within. I turned and headed for the stairs. Going upstairs in any house was always a risk, but it was one that often paid off. The steps were carpeted, which meant that I didn't have to be quite so careful about noise as I made my way up to the second floor.

In the hallway at the top, there was a large window that looked out onto the street. I could see the rain still beating down through the grey afternoon. Inside, four doors stood open, and I could see inside two of them from where I stood. Bedrooms. The beds had been stripped, though, just like in my house. I had no idea why Rifters needed so many sheets. *Maybe to hang themselves when they can't take living in hell anymore,* I thought. The darkness of the thought surprised me, though I didn't know why it should have. Life in the Rift Zone sucked. Was I supposed to be thinking about unicorns and rainbows?

"Rift kittens," Viktor whispered, suddenly at my side again. "Pink ones."

"I thought I told you to shut up."

"Since when do I listen?" He strode to the nearest door and leaned against the frame as he peered inside. "You *could* go back to Niesha's turf. I'm sure they have better stuff to steal."

"I don't know where all the caches are. Besides . . . Joshua's territory is closer."

He looked back at me with an amused quirk of his eyebrow. "What else to you have to do with your day? Walking over there would be good exercise."

"In case you haven't noticed, I'm not exactly taking in enough calories to be doing strenuous exercise."

He looked me up and down, and I thought something really annoying was going to come out of his mouth. Instead, he detached himself from the doorframe and walked back to where I stood at the top of the stairs. Sometimes he seemed so real. I could almost hear him breathing. I could almost *smell* him.

"Bet you never thought you'd miss that, did you?" he asked quietly. I pressed my lips into a thin line, trying to calm their quivering. "Hey. Léa. You're all right." He reached out as if he were going to pull me into a hug. But then he stopped.

"I just wish . . ." I began.

"You wish what?"

Taking a deep breath, I lifted my chin so I could look him in the eye. His good eye. "I wish I hadn't waited until the end to tell you how I really felt."

He tilted his head ever so slightly. "Did you even know how you really felt until then?"

"No." My voice was small. "I wouldn't let myself go there."

A small laugh escaped him, and he shook his head with a smile. "It's okay, Léa. I knew."

I opened my mouth to retort, but the words stuck in my throat as I heard the sound.

"What was that?" I whispered, realizing a moment later that I'd said the words out loud. The noise had come from the room at the end of the hall, which appeared to be a bathroom. Bracing my feet on the carpet, I raised my pinkhands and held my breath.

"You've got five seconds to get out of my way!" a female voice shouted. But she didn't even give me five seconds. A figure burst through the doorway, hands blazing. I jerked my right hand back, ready to throw . . . and stopped myself just in time.

"Holy shit," I breathed. I shook the Rift energy from my hands and let them fall to my sides.

Katja slowly lowered her glowing hands. "What the hell are you doing all the way up here?"

CHAPTER 7

REUNION

The greenish strip in her hair was long gone. It didn't look so great, anyway. It was stringy, pulled back into a loose bun. The hairstyle showed off gaunt cheekbones. She frowned and peered at me.

"I thought . . . So, you didn't go through with it?"

"Huh?"

"The scarring."

My hand rose automatically to my cheek. "Oh. I guess it didn't take."

She stared at me with wide eyes. "Are you serious?" Her gaze shifted behind me and down the stairs, as if she were looking for something. Or someone. "Are you alone?"

"Today, yeah." I jerked my chin toward the bathroom. "Is there anything in there?"

Her eyes narrowed ever so slightly. I let out a soft groan.

"Seriously? You're working for Joshua?"

"What? No." She shook her head and turned to gesture behind her, letting me catch a glimpse of the backpack that hung limp and empty from her shoulders. "Why would I want to work for someone who can't even keep a cache house stocked?"

"He spreads stuff out," I said absently.

"That's stupid."

"That's Joshua."

She grunted. "Are *you* working for Joshua?"

I gave her a look. "What do you think?"

"How should I know? Alliances are weird these days."

"Who's your alliance with?"

She paused for a moment as if weighing her options. Deciding whether to tell me. I shook my head.

"I know it's not Xavi. Definitely not Rasputin."

"Ryver," she said, which didn't surprise me much at all. "By the way, what the hell did you guys do? She's still pissed."

"Burned a cache. But it was one of Joshua's, and he's got plenty. Like I said . . . he spreads stuff out."

"You're working for him?"

The laugh burst out of me. I couldn't help it. "Seriously?"

"Well, you're awfully far from home if you're working for C-Roy. Besides . . . he doesn't need to steal anything. Or so I've heard."

I said nothing. Though I didn't exactly feel loyalty

to C-Roy, I didn't think he'd appreciate a flood of runners from other territories heading down there to steal from his apparently excellent stash.

"So, who is it?"

"I'm not working for anyone."

Her eyebrow rose.

"I'm here for myself, not some lazy boss who's afraid to get their own hands dirty."

"Sure." She took a step forward, her shoes silent on the carpet. "But you have to be living somewhere."

"A few blocks north of here."

"But . . ."

"But what?"

"That's Permanent Marc's territory."

"It's my old neighbourhood," I corrected her. "My old house."

"And he's left you alone?"

"So far," I lied.

She shook her head in disbelief. "I don't know if you're brave or stupid. Probably stupid."

"Why? I'm not afraid of a teenage boy with really bad taste in body art."

"Excuse me," she said, startling me with the venom in her voice. "Not everyone is okay with permanently scarring themselves. If we ever get out of here, I don't want to have to explain—"

"We're never getting out. And do I look like I've allied myself with Permanent Marc?" I asked, waving my hand at my forehead.

"You don't look like you've allied yourself with anyone."

"Like I said: I heal fast."

"What about Viktor and Click? Did they heal fast from Rasputin's little branding game?"

My throat tightened so much I didn't think I could speak. All I could do was shake my head. She frowned, then took another step forward.

"Léa?"

"It's okay," Viktor said, beside me once more, just when I least wanted the distraction . . . or the memory. "You can tell her. I trust her."

"We should've walked out of there with you," I choked out.

She shook her head. "What? I don't . . . Where are they?"

"Click's at home. With Buddy."

She waited, but when I didn't follow up with the third name, she got a little pale. Beside me, Viktor slipped his hand into mine. I could feel it . . . although it didn't feel quite right. It should've been warmer. Sweatier.

"Shit, Léa. Where's Viktor?"

"Gone," I whispered.

"Gone where?"

I shook my head. "He's dead," I managed to get out, even though my throat was doing its best to keep the words deep inside me. He squeezed my hand.

"What the fuck do you mean? How did . . . What happened? Did he get sick? Did Permanent Marc—"

"He killed himself."

Her eyes grew even wider. "What the hell? Viktor? Seriously . . . *Viktor?*"

I knew what she was trying to say, even if she couldn't articulate it. Turning to look out the window, I saw him out of the corner of my eye. Right there. And yet, so far away that it hurt my heart to think about it.

"Léa, what happened? Something must have happened, because he wouldn't have—"

"Rasputin—Charity—burned his eye," I said, turning back to face her. Her jaw dropped.

"Why?"

"She thought he was . . . someone else."

"Shit," she said, summing everything up succinctly. "His good eye, I'm guessing."

"Yeah."

"God, Léa. I'm sorry." She took another step closer, as if she were going to hug me. But, when I didn't move, she seemed to think better of it. "He didn't deserve that."

"She doesn't know," Viktor said. I frowned and tried to concentrate on the feeling of his hand in mine. "She doesn't know what I did."

"He seemed okay," I said, fixing my gaze on Katja's shoes. "I mean, not at first. But then . . . we were getting through it. He was making jokes again." I shook my head. "I guess he hid his pain really well."

She didn't ask any more questions. Not when. Not how. Not why. I wouldn't have had an answer for that last question, anyway. I still didn't know that answer myself.

"I need to get going," I said. "I don't want Click to worry."

She nodded. "Okay. Yeah." With a glance back at the bathroom, she frowned. "You want to search together and split what we find?"

"Will Ryver be okay with that?"

"How would she find out? Besides . . . old alliances have to be worth something in this place."

"See?" Viktor said, leaning down toward my ear. "Not everyone in this town is a batspit donkeybutt."

It was all I could do to keep from letting out a grunt of devastated laughter at his words.

—

By the time I made it home—with a bag of Cheeznudles and two single-serving bottles of pop tucked safely under my jacket—I was tired, soaked, and frustrated. Despite our best efforts, Katja and I hadn't been able to find much. Joshua probably thought he was being clever by hiding the meagre stash spread throughout the house. He didn't seem to realize that hungry people were perfectly willing to play hide-and-seek with junk food . . . even if the game was the most annoying one ever.

I went straight to the kitchen, Buddy at my heels, and dumped the stuff on the counter. Then I proceeded to shuck my shoes and peel off my sodden socks. The floor wasn't warm (it wasn't heated like the en suite floor in Viktor and Click's old place), but it still felt relatively toasty once I got my frozen feet out of their footwear hell.

"Click?" I called. Buddy let out a sharp bark, startling me. "Don't do that," I muttered. "He doesn't need to hear from both of us." A few seconds later, I heard Click's bouncy footsteps on the stairs. He walked into the kitchen, spied my finds, and let his face break into a smile. "Don't get too excited."

"Kah-tee," he said, and I shook my head, taken aback.

"Yeah . . . How did you know I ran into her?"

But he didn't answer. He walked straight to the pop, tapped his finger on the top of one of the caps, and looked at me hopefully.

"Guess you don't have this stuff in Reefa, eh?" Glancing at the clock on the stove, I sighed. "Time to start dinner. You want to help?"

He gave me a thumbs up, then went to the fridge. There wasn't much in there other than a few opened, half-empty cans. He got them all out and lined them up on the counter.

"Peaches, green beans, creamed corn, and black beans," I mumbled under my breath. "Damn it. If Joshua doesn't get his act together soon, I think I'm going to barf."

Click frowned, tilting his head.

"You know . . . Puke. Vomit. Hurl." I mimed the action, and his eyes widened in surprise. He quickly stepped forward and placed his hand on my stomach. "I'm fine," I said. "I'm just saying. We can't survive on this crap."

How the hell is Joshua doing it? I wondered. Although . . . maybe he wasn't. Teenage boys weren't known to be experts in nutrition. Still, if things were that bad in his territory, more kids would've been jumping ship.

"Maybe he distributes the real food and only caches the junk," I said, more to myself than anyone else. Click, whose hand was still on my stomach, raised his eyebrows. "He's got a checkpoint. So he's getting *some* decent stuff."

Click finally removed his hand and pointed at the bag of snacks.

"That's not decent. That's barely food." I sighed and grabbed the can of green beans, sliding it closer so I could peer inside. It looked about half full. "When I was a kid, I always wished we lived on the south side of Kenyonville. You know . . . down where C-Roy lives."

"See-rah."

"Exactly. I mean, those places aren't exactly mansions—there aren't any actual mansions in Kenyonville—but that was where the richer people lived. I thought it would be awesome to have a house with a pool."

He nodded like he understood exactly what I was saying. I didn't know if he did or not.

"I'm kind of wishing we lived down there right now. C-Roy's willing to share."

Click just stared at me expectantly as if he were waiting for an explanation.

"I couldn't stay. Not there." I shook my head slowly and stared at the dull green beans in their shadowy can. "I guess I could've asked him to set us up in another house, but . . ."

Click's gaze drifted down to my toes. I curled them against the floor.

"He might be willing to give us more food, but it takes hours to walk to his place, and we'd have to cross through other bosses' territories to get there. Either Joshua's and Ryver's or . . . Xavi's.

"Zah-vee."

"Yeah . . ." The idea started to percolate, crunchy bubbles of possibility in my mind. "Do you know where Niesha's old cache houses are?"

He gave me a thumbs up so quickly that I was sure he must've misunderstood. I shook my head and tried again.

"No, I mean . . . the places where Niesha stored the food. Other than the place you lived with Viktor."

His thumb was still in the air as he jabbed his fist forward.

"Shit."

"Lee-ah," he said, clearly admonishing me.

"Don't start channelling Viktor now," I muttered. "I can talk however I like. Besides, this is big. I just found out we could've been eating *real* food for the last couple of months."

He turned and plunged his fingers into the can of peaches, coming back with a syrupy piece that dripped on the counter and floor before he could get it to his mouth. Buddy immediately took care of the sticky drips on his level. I grabbed one of the old socks we'd been using as a dishcloth, wet it in the sink, and proceeded to clean the counter . . . all while my mind whirled with possibilities and plans.

CHAPTER 8

WHAT A DUMP

"Let's do this and get back to Buddy," I said as I hurried along Bower Avenue, the pink line to my left. The sidewalk on Joshua's side of the street seemed safer somehow, which was silly, considering we were eating and sleeping squarely on Permanent Marc's side of the line. I figured it was psychological. But knowing that didn't make me cross to the other side of the street. In fact, as soon as we reached Monroe, I led us south, farther into Joshua's territory. Click gently grabbed my arm, but I shook my head. "It's the scenic route."

He didn't argue, so we walked a few blocks down until we hit Havilland. The house—Buddy's old house—stood still and quiet. The giant lilac on the corner looked pretty pathetic without all its fragrant flowers. I paused for a moment, looking up at the porch. We knew this had been one of Joshua's caches.

Our last ill-fated attempt to scavenge had resulted in nothing but an inedible wristwatch. I wondered if Joshua had abandoned the place. Probably not. And, if he were smart, he would've beefed up security.

Joshua wasn't that smart, though, so I stood there for a long time, weighing our options. We were right there, after all. There might've been some good stuff. Then again, it was most likely on the second floor (or in the attic), and I had no idea who was guarding the place . . . or what kind of weapons they had. After everything we'd been through, pellet guns seemed quaint and laughable. But the guards would've been Rifters, too; just because they had pellet guns didn't mean they couldn't use their far more powerful built-in weapons.

Shaking my head, I turned away from the house and headed for the corner, then turned onto Havilland. Click kept pace with his bouncing gait, looking around as if he were taking in the scenery. As we moved farther down the street, though, all I could think about was that day, months earlier, when I'd taken that same route . . . in Viktor's arms.

"You're lucky I didn't drop you," he said.

"I'm not *that* heavy."

"Yeah, but you were lobbing pinkballs at the guys behind me."

"Don't call them that."

"Guys?"

"You know what I mean."

"Pinkballs? Why not? That's what they are." He jogged a little ahead so he could turn around and walk backward. I frowned. "What's wrong?"

"Are you going to keep popping in like this forever?"

He gave an exaggerated shrug, drawing his shoulders up toward his ears.

"How am I supposed to move on?"

"You *want* to forget me?" He sounded offended . . . but I couldn't tell if he was just pretending to be.

"I didn't say that."

With a thoughtful twist of his lips, he nodded. "You need closure."

"I need answers."

"We all need answers, Léa. That's, like, the human condition."

"I'd settle for one answer."

He just smiled. I could see he knew what I meant, but he wasn't offering what I wanted. It was like that day when he'd appeared to me in the garden, all frozen and glitchy when I'd tried asking him about the *why*.

"I know you were in pain," I said.

"Do you think that's the reason?" He thumped his chest with his fist and grunted. "I can handle pain."

"Okay, smartass. Then tell me."

He shook his head and turned around, leaving me staring at his back. His ponytail looked pretty loose. As if he could sense me thinking about it, he reached back and tightened it up.

"Vee-kah," Click said, jarring me back to reality. I turned to peer at him with a frown.

"How do you keep doing that?"

He tapped his fingers against his forehead, then pressed his hand against his heart. I sighed.

"I bet you miss him, too, don't you? He was your best friend."

"Bah-dee."

I let out a short laugh. "Don't tell Viktor."

Turning back to face the empty sidewalk ahead of us, I tried to focus on the job we were about to do. Niesha's old turf—Xavi's now—was pretty uninteresting as far as the territories went. It was all residential, save for a single, quaint corner store that had been ransacked in the early days. My experience with the area was limited to when I'd driven through it with my grandparents and the few excursions I'd gone on with Viktor and Click to grab stuff from the various caches. Each territory (well, the ones I was familiar with, anyway) seemed to have one central cache where food from the checkpoint was stored. Kids would drop by on a designated day to get what they could . . . which wasn't much. It was getting less as time went on, too. C-Roy probably had the right idea, figuring out a way to supplement what he was getting from the checkpoints.

"Where should we start?" I asked. Click turned to me expectantly. "The distribution cache? Or somewhere else?"

He stared at me for a moment as if he were listening, then quickened his pace. I walked a little faster to keep up and let him lead the way. After a few blocks, it was apparent that he was heading for the distribution cache. At least, it had been Niesha's distribution cache, the place where the runners had brought everything from the checkpoint so it could be sorted and handed out on Tuesday afternoons. Each checkpoint gave out supplies on a different day of the week. The variety also appeared to be different. Niesha's old turf had been heavy on dry goods like pasta, flour, and sugar, as if the checkpoint were supplying Rifters who liked to cook from scratch. Much of what I was pilfering from Joshua's turf seemed to be canned goods. Lots of beans. C-Roy had canned goods, too, but that was probably due to his other supply lines. Before, there had been quite a few MREs. Lots of freeze-dried, just-add-water stuff. He hadn't included any in the backpack he'd given us when we'd left a few months earlier, but I wasn't sure if that was because he was no longer getting those or if he'd thought lugging heavy cans all the way across town would be good for me.

As we approached the cache, I started to get nervous. I'd never been to this part of town at this time of year. The tree-lined streets looked bare and depressing, and there was an ominous sort of feeling that hung over everything. It didn't help that there seemed to be trash everywhere, which only added to the post-apocalyptic vibe. As I edged around an empty Cheeznudle bag that had gotten stuck on the bare branches of a shrub, I shook my head.

"Why aren't they taking the trash to the checkpoint? Niesha would be pissed."

Click slowed down long enough to point at a crushed and empty pop can in the gutter.

"Pigs," I muttered. But my unease was growing. If something as simple as trash disposal had been abandoned with Xavi's takeover, other things might have changed as well. "They might've abandoned the cache."

Click shook his head.

"How do you know?"

He stopped and pointed, this time up the street. I followed his finger with my gaze, spotting the movement. My first instinct was to jump into the bushes beside me. Since they were pretty bare of foliage, though, that wouldn't have done much. All I could do was stay as still as possible and hope not to draw any attention.

The two figures were arguing. I could see that. I could sort of hear it, too, though we were too far away to make out any actual words. Click and I stood there, silently, letting the bits of voice fly toward us like snippets of discarded plastic on the wind. The voices rose and fell, and even though the words were hard to make out, the anger wasn't. The emotional charge of the interaction became clear as pink flared in the distance.

"Shit," I whispered. Click glanced at me, but not in a chiding sort of way. He seemed to be looking to me for a cue. I just raised my hand, slowly so as not to draw too much attention.

Not that they would've noticed, anyway, because the next instant, a Riftball sailed between the two people and a very clear howl of pain skipped down the street toward us. Click started forward, no doubt to try to help, but I reached out and grabbed his arm. The last thing I wanted to do was get involved in . . . whatever this was. Audible swears echoed between the houses on either side of the street, and another Riftball lit up the day as it smacked into its target, hitting the kid squarely in the groin. Rift energy was worst when it hit the skin, but it was still pretty damn hot through fabric; I'd ended up with what looked like sunburn under my clothes a few times. I cringed as I thought about the burn that kid would be nursing later.

"That'll be a different kind of pinkballs," Viktor whispered in my ear.

"Shut up," I whispered back. Click turned to me with a frown, even though I hadn't actually spoken the words out loud. I glanced at Viktor, then shook my head. "You're going to distract me. If I end up burned to a crisp because of you . . ."

"I've seen your reflexes. You'll be fine."

"You've seen my startle reflex. That won't really help in this situation."

The two Rifters up the street were just standing

there. One was doubled over, hands pressed deep into his crotch. They appeared to be glaring at each other.

"Stalemate?" Viktor asked.

I had no idea. And I didn't really know what to do. I didn't want to just waltz down the street when they were still wound up. That would've been a recipe for pain. But we couldn't just stand there all day, either.

Luckily, I didn't have to worry about it for too long. The bent-over kid straightened up, both hands glowing. Click flinched.

"Holy spit," Viktor said, just as the two Riftballs launched. The other kid ducked, but one of the pink orbs hit him in the shoulder anyway, splattering like an overripe fruit, and he fell back on the pavement with a scream of pain. The assailant took the opportunity to flee, tripping over what looked like a bag of trash as he went; I heard the clatter of empty cans as the plastic broke and sent garbage spilling onto the street.

Click started to run.

I just stood there for a moment, thinking he was going after the kid who'd hurled the Riftballs. But then I understood.

"Click!" I hissed. When he didn't stop, I turned to Viktor. He raised his eyebrows.

"What?"

"He's going to get us killed."

He snorted. "By who? Niesha's ex-minions?"

"They have no loyalty to Niesha. Or Katja. Or

anyone with half a brain." I turned and frowned as I watched Click approach the kid who was still lying on the ground. "Damn it."

"He'll be fine. *You'll* be fine."

"Yeah. Sure."

"I'm serious, Léa. You can do this."

"Do what?" I asked, turning to face him. "Get myself fried by Xavi's crew? I'm sure I can."

He shook his head. "You're resourceful. Look at what you've already done."

"Got you blinded."

"I got myself blinded. Never mind that."

"Never *mind?*" I echoed.

"You survived in the Rift Zone by yourself for two years. And you've managed to keep Click alive for the last few months."

"Click eats like a bird. And he pretty much takes care of himself."

"You've kept yourself alive, too," he went on, "even though you're too stubborn to eat pine needles."

"You and your pine needles. Do you *like* those things or something?"

"They're an acquired taste."

"I'll say."

He gently touched my arm. "I wouldn't want you to have to chow down on any more needles, then. Go on. Find the cache. And then go straight home."

"I don't suppose you could tell me where the distribution cache is."

He gave me a little smile, twisting the bottom part of his scar. I turned away.

"Click!" I shouted, jogging toward him. There was no point in trying to be discreet now. Click had reached the Rifter and had crouched down beside him. I readied my hands, just in case . . . though it didn't look like the kid even noticed I was there. When I got a little closer, I saw that his eyes were screwed shut and he was panting.

"Fuck off," he said.

"Nice. Is that how you always treat people who are trying to help?"

He tried to open his eyes. They were watering like crazy. As he saw Click crouching beside him, he scrambled backward, seeming to forget about his injury for a moment. "Shit!" He stopped moving and let himself fall back against the pavement. "Motherfucking little—"

"Potty mouth," Viktor said, at my side once more. I chose to ignore him and crouched down opposite Click, who was tugging on the collar of the kid's t-shirt, trying to get a better view of the burn.

"Who was that who just tried to roast your head?" I asked. He stopped giving Click a nasty glare long enough to turn an incredulous expression on me.

"What's it to you?"

"I'd kind of like to know what the hell's going on here. This place is a mess."

"Yeah, well, that's what happens when little shitheads are left in charge."

I snorted. "From what I heard, nobody left Xavi in charge. He seized power."

The kid stared at me with this weird look. He seemed to be deciding whether to laugh or swear. Finally, he did both, sitting up and pushing Click's hands away.

"Let him help," I said.

"It's a first-degree Riftburn. I'm fine."

"You're lucky you were wearing a jacket."

"Yeah. Lucky." He tugged at the collar of his t-shirt, revealing the pink skin beneath. "I don't suppose you have any aloe."

"Oh, yeah. It's in my first-aid kit." I pretended to look around as I patted my pockets. He grunted and let go of his shirt.

"Where's Viktor?" he asked. I straightened up a little, taken aback. "Don't usually see him without that one." He jerked his chin at Click, who was frowning at the now-covered burn.

"He's dead," I said quickly. "So, who was the guy who nearly took off your head with a Riftball?"

"Shit." He held up his hand. "Viktor's dead?"

"Yeah. Who's the guy?"

"What the fuck?"

"Are you going to answer my question?"

"If you answer mine."

"I already did."

He looked at Click, then turned to me. "You're Léa?"

"Yeah . . ."

"Katja's nemesis?"

"Hardly."

He blew out a breath. His brow was still creased in pain, and tears stained his cheeks. He was young—younger than me, anyway—and still had that growing-teenage-boy sort of look to him. He hadn't grown into his nose and ears yet, and the skin under his wispy facial hair was pocked with angry-looking zits. A thought occurred to me with such suddenness and force that the swear escaped before I could stop it.

"Shit. Xavi?"

"Yeah." He let out a groan and got up, pushing Click's hand away once more. I stood quickly, noticing how the kid towered over me. He wasn't as tall as Viktor . . . but he was probably close.

"So you're the little pissant who staged a coup and let Niesha's whole territory go to shit?"

He turned to me with a dangerous look in his eye. *What the fuck, Léa? Are you trying to get yourself roasted?* I raised my chin and stared him down. He narrowed his still-streaming eyes.

"It wasn't a fucking *coup*," he said. "It was a democratic vote."

"So a bunch of morons voted you in. That makes it so much better."

"We didn't think Katja was doing enough."

"Enough of what?" I asked. Viktor leaned toward my ear.

"Stroking his ego, probably." He regarded Xavi for a moment, then sighed. "At least he's got a 'stache to be proud of."

I snorted before I could stop myself. Xavi gave me a weird look.

"We've been bleeding people for the last year. Niesha wasn't a great liaison with the checkpoint assholes, and a lot of us were tired of flour and sugar."

"Oh, god. You might have to cook something. The horror."

He gave me a dark look. "Those bastards weren't playing fair. This whole fucking town is one giant lab. Or did you not notice?"

"A lab?"

"Yeah. A giant science experiment. Except, unlike Cody Lamoreaux, those fuckers are actually *trying* to see how much they can mess up our lives."

My throat grew tight. I looked at Click, but he didn't seem to notice. He was watching Xavi talk, a weird intensity on his features. It almost looked like he was listening.

"That is true," Viktor said. "I wasn't *trying* to—"

"What do you mean?" I asked, trying very hard to ignore the ghost standing at my shoulder. Xavi sighed, the sound so weary that I was almost sorry I'd asked.

"Haven't you noticed the . . . uh . . . discrepancy? How each of the checkpoints hands out something different?"

"Yeah. So?"

"And the trash collection."

"What about it?"

He rolled his eyes as if he couldn't believe he was having to explain it. "We bring our trash to the checkpoints."

"Yeah. Have you seen a garbage truck in here for the last three-and-a-half years?"

"That's not why they want to see our trash. They're keeping track. Seeing how supplies move around in the Zone. If they get a bunch of empty cans from a territory that's only been given boxed food, then they can see where things are being traded."

"Why would they do that?"

"How the fuck should I know?" He gingerly rolled his shoulder, wincing as he did so.

"So . . . what? Are you paranoid or something? Why aren't you taking out the trash?"

"Because I'm not fucking in charge anymore." He shook his head. "Seriously? You think people in the Zone are stupid enough to throw Riftballs at bosses?"

I blinked. "You're not the boss?"

"No, I'm not the boss," he said, spitting the words. "I wouldn't be standing here having this fucking conversation with a stupid bitch if I were still a boss."

"Hey!" Viktor said. "Watch your mouth, donkeybutt."

"Why am I stupid?"

He stared at me for a moment, then shook his head. "Un-fucking-believable."

"Why am I stupid?" I repeated.

"Because you were *out*. You were fucking out, and you came back. At least Niesha had the brains to know a good thing when she saw it."

"Maybe we came back to help the rest of you."

He snorted. "Why the hell would you do that?"

"Because some people actually care about this town and the kids in it."

"Whatever. You know what I think? I think that melty-faced weirdo couldn't hack it on the outside. So he ran back in here to hide. You followed him. And we all know why you did that."

My mouth opened, but a response didn't emerge. It wasn't like Xavi was wrong. There probably had been an element of hiding on Viktor's part. Hiding from his past. From his family. From a world who blamed him for the Rift and a mini-apocalypse. I didn't know what to say. And the longer my silence hung in the air, the more solid the smirk on Xavi's face became.

"So, who was that?" I asked at last, gesturing to his shoulder. "The new boss?"

"Who'd want to be boss of this shithole?" He waved his hand in a sweeping arc.

"You. Or you wouldn't be so butthurt."

His eyes narrowed.

"Léa," Viktor murmured. "Be careful."

"You know what?" I said. "I really don't care. You're not the boss, and you don't seem to have any allegiance to whoever is. So, are you going to help us or not?"

He blinked, seemingly confused. "Help you what?"

"Rip off the distribution cache, for starters. We'll talk about the rest on the way there."

CHAPTER 9

THE OUSTED

Xavi didn't seem like he wanted any part of my plan, but he walked with us anyway, slightly ahead so he could lead, but not so far ahead that Click and I were at his back. He didn't trust us.

I didn't blame him.

The house where the Riftball fight had taken place was obviously not the distribution cache. It was probably *some* sort of cache, though, so I made a mental note of the house number when we went past, then focused on following the former boss up the street. It was actually pretty easy to tell which houses were occupied, even without the pink tickets, because trash had been left (stupidly) at the curb. There weren't many bags, either, so a lot of the garbage was loose. Empty cans rolled into the street. Cardboard boxes sat wet and flat after getting rained on. Niesha would've been appalled. Her house had been so tidy. At least until Joshua's goons had burned it down.

At the corner, Xavi turned left. He didn't seem to be slowing down at all, which struck me as kind of foolhardy if he really had been ousted. I started to wonder if we were walking into some sort of trap, and I almost grabbed Click's arm to hold him back.

"You're almost there," Viktor said. "Might as well see it through to the end."

"Yeah. But it better not be *my* end."

He snorted. "Xavi's a donkeybutt. But he's not batspit like some of the other people in this town."

I turned to him with a frown. "How the hell do I know that?"

"I'm telling you."

"Yeah, but you're just a figment of my imagination."

His eyes widened. "*Really?*"

"Shut up."

"Maybe you just have a really good gut instinct."

"I shouldn't be trusting Xavi at all. He's the reason we had to go down to Rasputin's turf, remember? If Katja hadn't been kicked out—"

"Right. Forgot about that."

"You forgot about Rasputin?"

"Wouldn't *you* want to block out something like that?"

"How do you know what you're blocking out if you've blocked it out?"

He laughed and veered closer so he could throw his

arm around my shoulders. I could almost feel it. God, I could almost feel it, and I just wanted to cry. "Hey. Léa. You're all right."

"You keep saying that. But I'm not."

"Maybe you are."

"And maybe Click and I are walking into a deadly trap."

"If that's the case, I'll prepare myself to hear the 'I told you so' to end all 'I told you sos' . . . okay?"

"I don't particularly want to die today."

"Good thing you're not going to." He pulled away just as I looked up and saw that Xavi had stopped in front of the second house from the corner. It looked much like many of the other houses in that area: two storeys, mature gardens, and wooden fences. This particular fence looked awful, though.

"Where are Rifters getting spray paint?" I asked, peering at the gaudy orange tag.

"It doesn't go bad," Xavi said. "It's probably been in the town since before the Rift." He gestured toward the house. "Well, there it is."

"Okay."

"Thought you wanted to rip it off."

"You think I'm going to walk in there ahead of you?"

He grunted. "You think I'm going to walk in there ahead of *you?*"

"Someone has to go first."

I should've known what was about to happen, even before Click pushed past us and scampered up the walk to the porch steps. Xavi watched him for a moment, then turned to me.

"He stupid or something?"

"He's probably smarter than either of us." I shook my head and waved my hand. "You going to go?"

"We need some rules."

"Like what?"

"I get half."

I snorted. "Ripping off an entire cache at once is a pretty damn stupid strategy."

"If your strategy is so smart, why do you look like you're about to keel over from starvation?"

"Because the shit in Joshua's territory is awful. You'd look like crap, too, if you'd been constipated for a week due to a Cheeznudle overdose."

He snorted. "They still make those things?"

"As far as I know. Either that, or they're just funnelling the expired stock into the Rift Zone and expecting us to . . . process it."

"Process it. Nice."

"Not really."

With a shake of his head, he stepped toward the house. Click was already on the porch, waiting for us.

"So, who lives here?" I asked. Xavi just shrugged. I gaped at him. "What do you mean?"

"Things change fast."

"I'll say."

"There wasn't anyone living here when I was in charge."

"Smart."

He gave me a dark look. "I *had* someone in here, but they skipped town."

"What?"

"Skipped territory. Whatever. Last I heard, she was going to try her luck with C-Roy."

Unless she's missing a toe, she probably won't have much luck, I thought. The food situation might've been better down south . . . but C-Roy was going to want to keep it that way. And taking in too many refugees wouldn't help.

"Well?" Xavi said. "You going in, or what?"

"After you."

He snorted. "How fucking stupid do you think I am?"

"You got into a Riftball fight in a town without a proper hospital. So . . . pretty damn stupid."

"That was self-defence."

"Looked like a low blow to me."

"Whatever." He grabbed the doorknob, gave it an angry twist, and shoved the door open. But he didn't step inside.

"Is there anything in there?"

"How the hell should I know?"

I gave him a look. He shook his head.

"I'm not in charge anymore. I don't know what the distribution situation is. Hell, I'm lucky I haven't been run out of town yet."

"Why haven't you?"

"I probably will be now." He ran a hand back

through his hair. It was straight and sort of a colour-less brown. And it looked like it had been chewed to its current length by a couple of hungry piranhas. "At least I'm smart enough to get the hell out of . . ."

"What?"

He shook his head again. "Never mind."

"Like hell. You don't just drop cryptic hints. This isn't a badly written novel. This is our life. Withholding important information just to seem mysterious is—"

"Fuck, Léa. I'm not." He regarded me for a long moment. "You *really* want to know what's going on here?"

"Yeah . . ." I said, drawing the word out so much that it sounded like it had the opposite meaning. I sighed. "Just tell me. It can't be any worse than what I'm imagining."

"Permanent Marc's cult has taken over."

Okay. It's worse.

"Spit," Viktor breathed. He was standing just behind my left shoulder, close enough that I felt slightly comforted, even though Xavi's words had poured a metaphorical bucket of ice water right over my head. I shuddered.

"Taken over how?" I asked. "Why didn't anyone fight back?"

"Because he's running a fucking cult. And after three years of this shit, people are easy prey."

I shook my head. "What's he promising them?"

"Hell if I know."

"Then how do you know—"

"Because he sent his recruiters over here. I didn't want to listen, but some of the others did."

"Crystal?" I asked, trying to remember the few names I could recall from Niesha's old workforce. "Draven?"

"Among others." He frowned as he peered into the house through the open door. It was dark in there, but reassuringly quiet. "It was my fault. I thought we should have a democracy. Everybody got a vote. Didn't think they'd all vote to let themselves be annexed."

I blinked. "What?"

"Yeah. Officially, you're in Permanent Marc's territory." He reached up and rubbed his hand over his forehead, as if he were thinking of those scars that marked Permanent Marc's followers.

"So what are you still doing here?" I asked, just as Click—who had been bouncing on the balls of his feet, waiting for us to make a decision about entering the house—stepped across the threshold. "Click! Don't."

"It's fine," Xavi said. "Let him."

"Maybe you don't care about anyone but yourself, but—"

"Seriously? That's pretty rich, coming from you."

"Excuse me?"

"You didn't seem to care about taking Niesha out of here, leaving us with this mess. Leaving Katja heartbroken."

I just gaped at him. "Are you serious? What makes you think I had any say in the matter?"

"You come and go as you please. So you're obviously batshit. Nobody with two brain cells to rub together would come back here." He waved his hand as I opened my mouth to speak. "Give me a break, Léa. Nobody would willingly come back into the Rift Zone. Not unless there was something in it for them."

"You got me. I just couldn't get enough expired Cheeznudles."

"That's not what I'm talking about."

"Yeah, I know. Look, I didn't know about Katja's crush. I don't even know if Niesha knew about it. As for leaving, that was one-hundred percent Niesha's idea. So don't you dare blame me for that. I came back. Fine. But that doesn't mean anything that happened over here is my fault. *You* let your stupid territory get taken over by Permanent Marc. That's not my problem."

His eyes narrowed. "Over here?"

"What?"

"Where the hell are you living?"

"Where do you think?" I snapped.

"Judging by your smooth forehead . . ."

Shaking my head, I peered into the darkness of the house. "Click, come on. We're going."

"I thought you wanted to rip this place off," Xavi said.

"I'm not ripping off Permanent Marc. Are you insane?"

"We're all insane." He ran his fingers through his

hair again, leaving some of it standing straight up. "He hasn't gotten a strong foothold yet. Only a few kids have taken the mark."

"They *what?*"

"Yeah. Cult initiation. Whatever." He shook his head. "My point is that they haven't sorted out the logistics yet. Some of our old caches have been abandoned. I don't know if that's because there's some sort of consolidation going on, or if they're just really unorganized. But this"—he waved his hand toward the shadowy interior—"might be our last chance to grab whatever's left. Before they beef up security."

I chewed on my lip for a few seconds. I could feel Viktor still standing at my back, not saying anything. Probably because I didn't know what to say, either. I didn't know what to do. The thought of finding something good was certainly tempting, but the last thing I wanted to do was piss off Permanent Marc. Especially when I was technically living in his territory. I didn't know why there hadn't been a followup visit from one of his lackeys. Maybe he'd forgotten about us.

I certainly didn't want to do anything to make him remember.

"It's really not that difficult," Xavi said. "You either want what's in there, or you don't. If you don't, that just leaves more for me."

"It's not that simple," I snapped. "I don't even know you. For all I know, this could be a trap. You could hand me over to Permanent Marc. And we all know what happens to people who cross him."

"Those are rumours. Bullshit ones."

I shook my head and squeezed my eyes shut as a horrible vision flashed across the movie screen of my memory. Viktor laid a gentle hand on my shoulder.

"You're all right," he whispered.

"They're not bullshit," I said, opening my eyes to glare at Xavi. "You want to come over to my old place and see the bloodstains?"

He snorted. "You look fine to me."

"I wasn't the target." Turning, I pressed one hand against the doorframe and leaned inside. "Click! Come on." But the boy didn't appear. With a grating sigh, I stepped over the threshold and into the house.

CHAPTER 10

SACRIFICE

"Whew. Stinks in here," Viktor said. I couldn't argue. It definitely smelled like something had gone bad in the fridge. The hallway was kind of dark, but I didn't bother with the light switch. I just lit one hand and stepped toward the back of the house. Toward the smell.

Click was already crouched in front of the open fridge door, pawing through what was left in one of the crisper bins. I retched before I could stop myself, and the sound echoed in the empty space. Xavi chuckled.

"What?" I snapped. "You *like* that smell?"

"I'm *used* to that smell." He stepped closer to the open fridge, leaning one hand on the door as he peered down into the lit interior. "Beans smell like farts, even when you've just opened the can. Some people don't bother eating the rest."

"So they leave them in the fridge to rot? Bright."

He glanced back at me, eyebrow quirked. "You think a town full of teenagers is supposed to be bright?"

"Aren't you a teenager?"

"Yeah. And I've grown up way too fast." He grabbed Click's arm and pulled him to his feet. I took a step back.

"Go wash your hands," I muttered, pointing at the sink. There was a soap bottle there. *It's probably too much to ask that there's something in it, though.* He obliged without an argument, and Xavi slammed the fridge door shut.

"You probably weren't after leftovers anyway, were you?" he asked.

"Were you?"

"Fuck, no. Especially not those ones."

"So where's the rest of the stuff?" I asked, eyeing the cupboards. They were all closed, which was both a promise and a tease. Xavi saw where I was looking, grabbed a brushed nickel handle, and paused for an instant before throwing the door open, almost like he was afraid he was about to be beset by bats (or something equally as creepy). But all that greeted us was a very empty cupboard. He quickly checked the one beside it, but that was empty, too. I sighed.

"Were you really expecting to find a treasure trove of food? Checkpoint day is on Monday. Distribution day is on Tuesday. Even *if* there had been something here yesterday, it's gone now."

"Monday?" I echoed.

"Yeah. Each checkpoint hands out food on a different day."

"I know that."

He had all the cupboards—all the empty cupboards—open. With a sour expression, he began to close them, one by one, with a series of bangs that made me wince. "So now Permanent Marc's got two checkpoint days. Twice as much food."

"Twice as many people to feed," I pointed out.

"Maybe more. Sounds like his cult is growing."

I shook my head. Out of the corner of my eye, I could see Viktor frowning. "I don't believe it," I said. "Rifters might be dumb. But not *that* dumb."

"What's 'that dumb'?" Xavi asked, the last word almost drowned out by another slamming cupboard door.

"Permanently scarring themselves just to join a silly club. What if they get out of here one day? Who's going to hire someone who's done *that* to their face?"

He straightened up and turned to me, a look of disbelief plastered across his features. "You seriously think we're ever getting out of here?"

"Why wouldn't we?"

"Um, hello? The Rift?" He waved his arm in a westerly direction. "As long as that's there—and affecting us—we're not going anywhere."

"Have you forgotten that we found a way out?"

"Yeah. And you came back into this shithole. So

you'll excuse me if I view anything you say as pretty fucking stupid."

I watched him for a moment. Finally, I narrowed my eyes.

"I don't like you, either," he said.

"What the hell? I didn't say anything."

"You didn't have to." He stepped past the fridge, and past Click, who was still standing by the sink. He hadn't washed his hands yet. I gave him a pointed look, and he turned to the water.

"Was the food *only* stored in the kitchen?" I asked as Xavi disappeared into the next room without a word. Which was most likely my answer. But I didn't want to follow him deeper into the house (I didn't know him very well, after all), so I waited until Click finished. As I'd suspected, there was no soap. He shook his hands off, then wiped the excess water onto his denim jacket. "Want to help me check upstairs?" I asked, which earned me a thumbs up. With a little smile, I turned back toward the stairs, holding my glowing hand out in front of me for light. What I could see of the living room as we passed it wasn't entirely unexpected. It looked like most of the furniture was still there, although it had been pushed and stacked around the perimeter of the room, almost like someone had been making space for something. I didn't doubt that food distribution had run a lot smoother when Niesha was in charge. They'd probably stored whatever they could get in that room.

The carpet on the stairs was still plush, and I longed to take off my shoes so I could feel the soft pile. But it was also pretty dirty, like a whole horde of zombies had traipsed upstairs without bothering to take their shoes off. If the owners ever did come back, they would have to get the carpet steam-cleaned . . . or replaced.

"Niesha's no-shoes policy didn't extend to the distribution cache," Viktor said. He was already at the top of the stairs when I got up there, leaning one hand against the white railing. I ignored him as I poked my head into the bathroom. "Wanna see if the floors are heated?"

"Click," I said, gesturing down the hall, "check the room at the front of the house. I'll check the other two."

He nodded and tiptoed lightly across the carpet, his sandals making no noise at all. I pushed open the door that was closest to me, revealing what was once a child's bedroom. *Probably too young to be a Rifter*, I thought as my gaze skimmed over the painted unicorn mural on the wall behind the rather small bed. *Lucky kid.*

I pulled that door closed before turning to the last room, which was also a bedroom. This one, though . . . It was hard to tell how old its occupant had been. There were a couple of posters of racing cars still on the walls, and the lamp on the bedside table was in the shape of a vintage motorcycle. Whoever it was who had lived here, they'd liked things that went fast . . .

though that didn't really clear up the age or gender of the occupant.

"Probably ended up in the care of the aid orgs," Viktor mumbled, leaning over my shoulder to peer inside the room.

"You don't know that."

"It's a fair guess. Any younger, and they probably would've had a race-car bed."

I pressed my lips together and stared at the lamp.

"The group homes weren't *that* bad."

"Then why did you leave?"

He said nothing. I edged away from him and headed down the hall to the front room. As I stood in the doorway, I saw Click pawing through a chest of drawers that, somehow, hadn't already been ransacked.

"Anything to eat?" I asked, at which he turned to me and held up a pair of skimpy-looking panties.

"Are they edible?" Viktor asked.

"Shut up."

"Oh, come on. You really expected me not to go there?"

I shook my head and stepped over to the window at the front of the house. The street looked lifeless. The trees were bare, the sky was grey, and the light that managed to make it through the cloud cover did little to brighten up the afternoon.

So when I spotted the flash of bright pink, I snapped to attention.

"Oh, spit," Viktor said, but I'd already ducked

down, out of view. My first instinct was to tell him to do the same, before remembering that I was the only one who could see him.

"Click!" I hissed. He turned to me just as I heard the voices.

Right outside the house.

Coming up onto the porch.

"Zah-vee," he said, but I just shook my head. I very nearly put my glowing finger to my lips, but stopped myself just in time. My heart was pounding so hard that I didn't trust myself with pinkhands at that moment, so I shook the glow away and crawled over to where Click was standing by the dresser. I grabbed his hand and tugged him down to the floor. Below us, the voices rose as the Rifters entered the house.

"Holy shit!" a male voice said. "Is there a stinker in here?"

"Not unless someone died and started rotting in the last few hours." The second voice was higher. It might've been a girl. But it might've been a teenage boy.

"It's just something in the fridge," a third voice— unmistakably deep and male—said. I heard the front door close . . . and I wondered if Xavi had heard it, too. Glancing at Click, I crawled toward the bedroom door and started to push it closed. There wasn't any food upstairs—not unless it was hidden really well—so the trio probably wouldn't have a reason to make the climb. I didn't want to give them one by alerting them to our presence. But when the door hinges let out a squeak, I stopped, my breath locked.

"What the fuck are we doing here again?" the higher voice asked. "Besides gagging, I mean."

"Cleaning it out," the deep voice said. "The boss wants it done by next Monday."

"It's not going to take that long."

"Wanna bet? These morons obviously don't know what the hell they're doing. You don't let food go *bad* in the Zone. That's just disrespectful." There was a soft thud that I recognized as the suction of an opening fridge door. "Shit."

The higher voice laughed. "I thought you were cleaning it out."

"No, *you* are cleaning it out."

There was a grumble. I sat there, my knees digging into the carpet, as I listened to the sounds coming from the kitchen. The rest of the house appeared to be empty—of food, anyway—and it definitely wasn't going to take three people to clean out what was in the fridge. Glancing back at Click, I noticed him frowning, his head slightly cocked.

"What?" I mouthed, but when he opened his mouth to say something, I shook my head so forcefully that he didn't speak. I'd never heard the guy whisper, and I didn't want him to give away our presence.

"Hurry up," the deep voice said. "We've got four more to get through after this."

"Is that all?" the higher voice asked. Now that I'd heard it a few more times, I was pretty sure it was a girl.

"For today."

There was a groan.

"Want to rephrase that?"

"Shit, man," the first voice said. "You try getting your 'nads fried and see how *you* like walking all over town."

"First, your junk is fine. Second, we're not walking all over town. It's a few fucking blocks. Third, if you're not with us—"

"I am," the first voice said quickly. He almost sounded afraid.

"Good. Then finish up here. I'll sweep the rest of the—"

There was suddenly a lot of swearing and shouting. I grabbed the door in my panic and almost slammed it shut before I caught myself.

"What the fuck?" someone yelled. I honestly couldn't tell which of the guys it was. "Are you serious?"

"I am when you're taking over one of my caches." The new voice was familiar.

"Spit," Viktor whispered. "Is that Xavi?"

"It's not *yours*," the girl said. "We voted. Remember?"

"Yeah, I remember," Xavi said. "Disloyal little shit."

"Seriously, Xavi? Did you think things were going *well* on this side of town?"

"Well, they weren't so bad that you all needed to run off and join a cult."

The owner of the deep voice laughed. "A cult? Really?"

"You brand yourselves, swear loyalty to a batshit leader, and jerk off in front of a rip in the spacetime continuum. If that's not a cult . . ."

There was silence downstairs. I held my breath, straining to hear something. Anything. And when I did . . . I wished I hadn't.

As the gunshot continued to echo in my head, my hands flew automatically to my ears, even though they were too late to do anything. A scream echoed up from the first floor, genderless and terrified. I couldn't tell who it belonged to.

"What the fuck?" the girl shouted, so loudly I could hear her past my hands. "What the fuck?"

A second shot rang out, followed by silence. My hands still pressed over my ears, I looked up at Viktor, who was standing like a statue by the window.

"You're all right," he said, even though he didn't sound too sure. "You're—" But he broke off as Click jumped toward the door, grabbed the knob, and wrenched it open. I grabbed his leg—which was the closest thing I could reach—then his skirt, then his jacket, trying to hold him back. I wanted to tell him to stop, but I didn't dare . . . and he was intent on getting out of that room, seemingly intent on going downstairs, and I had no idea why. Until I thought about it.

No, I thought. *Click, you can't. If you go down there . . . they're going to kill us, too.*

He pried at my fingers, trying to make me let go. I scrambled to my feet, grateful for the carpet that muffled my movements, and grabbed him firmly by the arm. As I started to haul him over to the closet, he opened his mouth. I slapped my hand over it. The sound was sharp. I froze, trying to listen, but all I could hear was the beating of my heart in my ears. The voices started up again downstairs.

"Are you *trying* to make more work for us? Jesus Christ, Topher. What's wrong with you?"

"You think he was ever going to go along with it?" Topher asked. His voice was weirdly high, and he seemed to be panting. "I had to."

"No," the girl said. "You wanted to. Fuck. Fuck, fuck, fuck!" She sounded like she was near tears. I took the opportunity while they were talking to start pulling Click toward the closet again. He resisted, but it was almost like he was fighting with himself, unsure whether to listen to me or listen to his instinct . . . which I suspected was to help Xavi. I pulled open one of the double doors, grateful when it didn't squeak, and shoved Click inside. I squeezed in with him, pulling the door closed, and stood there, blocking his way out.

I couldn't hear much from downstairs. Just snippets of voices that leaked through the space between the closet doors. There were a few thumps, including a large one that shook the house. The front door? Click eventually stopped trying to get past me. He sank down onto the floor of the closet and started to cry. At least, that was what it sounded like. All I could hear was sniffling reminiscent of the time when we'd almost gotten his little canine friend turned into dinner. Carefully, I got down on my knees and leaned forward, groping in the darkness until I found his hunched form and gathered it into a hug.

"I'm sorry," I whispered. "I know you wanted to help him. But . . . I don't even know if you could have."

He returned the hug, his fingers digging into my back. "Ree-fah," he said softly, his voice above a whisper, but not so loud that I worried about anyone hearing.

"I know you want to go home. I know. I'm sorry. I'm so sorry, Click."

"I'm sorry, too," Viktor said. "Tell him I'm sorry for trapping him in this heckhole."

I shook my head and pulled away. The closet was filled with the sound of our breaths and the faint scent of my panicked sweating.

"Léa, tell him."

"No," I snapped. "You don't apologize for this. It was *not* your fault."

"Xavi was a donkeybutt, but he didn't deserve—"

"None of us deserve to be here. Except maybe Permanent Marc. Or Rasputin. Or Topher." I had no idea who Topher even was, beyond the fact that he'd gotten into a Riftball fight with Xavi earlier. All I knew was that he had a gun—a real one—and he wasn't afraid to use it.

"None of you would be here if it wasn't for what I did."

"Shut up!" I shouted at him. Even though the

words didn't actually leave my lips, Click jerked as if he'd been startled. "All I have left is the memory of you. Don't try to ruin it, Viktor. Please. Let me remember you as . . ."

I expected him to say something, but my mind remained as quiet as the house.

And the house remained quiet for hours until I finally worked up the courage to open the closet door. The sun had set, so I lit both hands and led us out of the bedroom, nudging the door open with my foot. Something told me we should go straight to the front door, out into the night, and not stop walking until we got home. But I had to know. So as soon as we'd tiptoed down the stairs, I stepped back toward the kitchen, holding my hands in front of me for light.

The floor was empty. All that remained was a slight, streaky smear of darkness where someone had done a shitty job of cleaning up.

"Zah-vee," Click said, the sadness in his voice almost more than I could bear. I turned and looked at him, watching the pink glow flicker on his twisted features.

"I'm sorry," I said, even though I didn't know what I was apologizing for. Not letting us get ourselves killed along with Xavi?

The Rift Zone could really mess with a person's head.

CHAPTER 11

CHRISTMAS

According to C-Roy's calendar, there were only two more days until Christmas . . . and I desperately wanted—no, needed—a distraction. All I'd been able to think about for the past couple of weeks was what had happened at the distribution cache. Etched on the screen of my mind was that smear of blood on the kitchen floor, taking its place among the other images from the Rift Zone mental-photography collection: the dark stain on the headrest of Grandpa's chair, Buddy's owner's half-eaten face, Carrick Frazier counting down the last days of his life in a medically induced coma, Viktor writhing in pain as Rasputin pressed her thumb against his eye . . . Viktor standing in the alley behind Dr. Bryan's office with his hands menacingly aglow . . . Viktor stepping out in front of a semi in the darkness and rain, putting an end to a life that he no longer saw the value of. Of course, that last one was merely what I imagined. But it felt as real as the others.

My imaginings were getting pretty damn real.

"Think we'll get a white Christmas?" Viktor asked as he stood by the front window and peered out through the narrow gap between the curtains. I hadn't opened them up yet, so the room was a bit dim, lit only by the ugly fixture that hung from the ceiling in the corner of the room. Not that the living room would've been much brighter with the curtains open. The day was a gloomy one, rainy and grey. I could feel the cold, wet air trying to seep through every window frame. Grandma had been on Grandpa's case for years about those windows, begging him to replace them with something more energy efficient. Grandpa had kept saying he'd get on it . . . but he never had, and when Grandma had gotten sick, the idea had been abandoned completely. Now, I was wishing he'd done something about it. Don't get me wrong: I was grateful to have a house—an intact, relatively comfortable house—in the Rift Zone. We had electricity to run the fridge, stove, washer and dryer, and lights; running water to keep us hydrated and clean; and warmth . . . although the baseboard heaters really did need a good cleaning since they smelled like burning dust every time I cranked up the heat. Grandma had periodically vacuumed them to get out the dust and spider carcasses. I hated to think what I would've found inside them after so many years of neglect.

I was curled up on the loveseat, close to the light of

the lamp so I could see well enough to read one of Grandpa's old paperbacks. Buddy was next to me, snuggled against my butt, as close as he could get. It didn't seem possible that he was cold, but maybe he was . . . and I apparently had the warmest rear end. Click didn't appear to mind Buddy's heat-seeking behaviours, though. He sat on the floor, slowly working his way through a 500-piece jigsaw puzzle that I'd found in the attic. I didn't remember it, but it was probably one of Grandma's; I certainly wasn't interested in doing a puzzle of a bunch of lap dogs dressed as military officers.

"It could snow," Viktor said, turning around to face me. I shook my head.

"It won't."

"It *could.*"

"Fat chance."

He grunted in amusement and sat down on the cushionless half of the loveseat. Buddy didn't notice, even when Viktor reached out and scratched behind the dog's ears. "Did you celebrate Christmas?" he asked. I frowned. "Oh. Sorry. Jewish?"

"No."

"Muslim?"

"No."

"Atheist?"

I screwed up my nose. "Not really."

He nodded sagely and leaned back with a sigh. "It's hard to know what to believe anymore, isn't it?"

"Are we still talking about religion?"

"I don't know. Are we?"

I turned back to my book. But it was hard to concentrate with a persistent ghost sitting just inches away.

"So? Did you celebrate Christmas?"

"Yeah. You saw the stuff in the attic."

"Right. So . . . why aren't you celebrating it now?"

With a sigh, I pulled my attention away from the page (which obviously wasn't holding my interest, anyway) and turned to him. "What's there to celebrate?"

"I don't know. Looks like a pretty cozy scene to me." He glanced at Buddy, then looked over at Click, who was sliding a long strip of pieces across the floor, rearranging some rather large patches of colour. Unlike Grandma, who'd always done the edges first, Click seemed to be saving those for last. "The happy couple and their dog," Viktor added, and the ridiculousness of his words made me snort.

"Shut up."

"What?"

"We're not a couple."

"You could do worse than Click."

"And Click could do better than me."

"Nope. Not possible."

I felt my cheeks grow warm, but Viktor wasn't done yet.

"He'd make pretty babies."

"Shit, Viktor. I don't even know if he likes girls. I don't know if he likes . . . anyone. And, even if he did, that's the last thing he should be worrying about."

"Kind of hard to do the RZRA without—"

"If I wouldn't repopulate the Zone with you, what makes you think I'd do it with him?"

He laughed, surprising me. But I wasn't amused. I was just annoyed. And he could see it. "Oh, come on, Léa. You should know by now that I'm just teasing."

"Do you have to?"

"Probably. It's some sort of congenital defect that makes me—"

"Oh, my god. Shut up." I snapped the book closed. Buddy jerked, aroused from his nap. Click didn't look up, though; he was too engrossed in his puzzle. I set the book aside and stood. Carefully stepping over the spread-out puzzle pieces, I headed for the stairs.

"Lee-ah."

"I'm just going up to the attic," I said. "You don't have to come."

But, a moment later, he came trailing up the stairs after me. So did Buddy. When I yanked on the cord, the hatch swung down from the ceiling, and I carefully unfolded the ladder. We climbed up into the attic while Buddy whined from below.

"Stay there," I said, peering down through the hole at the little white dog who had his front paws on the first rung as he looked up at me. He let out a whiny, angry bark. "Buddy. Stay!" He scratched at the rung, almost as if he were about to try to climb the ladder. I held my breath. But he gave up soon enough with another noise that clearly communicated his indignation at being left below.

"Bah-dee," Click said, but I shook my head.

"He's fine. Come over here," I said, crawling to the Christmas stuff on my hands and knees. "You want to do Christmas?"

"Yes!" Viktor said, suddenly (and predictably) in the attic with us. I looked back over my shoulder to see the top half of him as he stood on the ladder, leaning his elbows on the floor and smiling at me. Click approached, looking confused.

"Do you celebrate Christmas in Reefa?" I asked, which just earned me a blank look. So I tugged on the flaps of the cardboard box, revealing the plastic needles of the artificial pine tree. "Christmas?" I tried again. He trailed his fingers along the soft green spikes, listening to the whisper of the plastic.

"Guess that's a no," Viktor said. "We'll have to teach him."

"With what?" I asked. "A plastic tree and a few ornaments?"

"Presents. Christmas dinner. Egg nog."

I snorted. "Where the fuck am I supposed to find egg nog?"

"Good point."

"I haven't even seen an egg in over three years."

"Another good point. But I'm sure you can whip up something for dinner. You're getting really good at making edible food out of crap."

I smiled in spite of myself. "What a recommendation."

"I'm serious! I would totally eat it if . . . you know."

"If you weren't dead?"

He didn't say anything. When I looked back at the hatch, I saw that it was empty.

—

It took both me and Click to get the Christmas tree box down the ladder. Then I just let it slide down the stairs like a toboggan. I didn't remember it being so heavy; then again, Grandpa had always dealt with the thing. I was pretty impressed that he'd been able to do it on his own.

Setting up the tree didn't take very long at all, and I soon had the coloured lights strung on the branches, evenly spaced. Buddy seemed to be fascinated, and I worried for the first half hour that he was going to lift his leg on the painted trunk. But he didn't. Eventually, he gave up sniffing and just sat down and stared at the tree as if he couldn't get enough of the pretty coloured lights.

Click wasn't much different. As I returned from the attic with the box of ornaments, I found him sitting next to Buddy on the floor, the lights reflecting like rainbow fireflies in his golden irises.

"We're not done yet," I said, carefully setting the plastic box on the floor. I knelt next to it and opened the lid. Our ornaments were nestled within, most of them wrapped in tissue paper, but a few (like basic glass baubles) were safely sectioned in cardboard boxes. I took the tissue-wrapped pieces out and handed them to Click, who set the ornaments aside with a confused frown. "They go on the tree," I said. His frown deepened. I pointed at the tree. "We hang them on the branches. Just like the lights." He looked at the pile of tissue next to him, then at the tree. At last, his face relaxed. "Understand?" He gave me a thumbs up.

Buddy supervised as Click and I carefully unwrapped and hung each ornament. A rush of nostalgia came flooding back as I handled the precious memories and watched them swing gently from the fake pine boughs. Grandma had bought me a new ornament every year, up until the year she'd gotten sick, so there were sixteen of my ornaments to be hung . . . everything from a transparent acrylic snowman to a carved wooden squirrel holding a comically large acorn in its little paws. When all my ornaments were up, we finished decorating with the delicate glass balls. Soon, the tree was looking like a real symbol of the holidays. The colourful lights glittered and shone, reflecting on some of the ornaments, making the living room feel like a cozy haven. For a few moments, I even forgot we were in the Rift Zone, locked in a post-apocalyptic hell where angry kids hurt each other because they had no power to do anything else.

When we were done, I gathered up all the tissue paper and stuffed it back in the plastic bin. Click sat silently, staring at the tree with a little smile on his face, his fingers absently massaging Buddy's ears. I joined him on the hard floor, hugging my knees as I gazed up at the tree. It looked pretty good, aside from the fact that there was no tree-topper (Grandma's special angel hadn't been in the box). The normalcy soothed me, and I felt some of my worries start to recede a little. They didn't go far—there was still plenty to be concerned about—but I was able to forget them for a few moments.

"Wish we had some Christmas music," I said. Click turned to me, his eyebrows raised. "I'm not usually a fan," I went on, "but I kind of miss it now." The radio in Grandpa's truck sprang to mind, and I got excited for a moment. There was always some radio station playing nothing but Christmas music at this time of year. But then I remembered that nobody had started the truck for over two years . . . so the battery was probably good and dead. I sighed.

"You could always sing," Viktor said, strolling into the room and pausing beside the tree as he looked it up and down. "Nice."

"I'm not singing."

"Why not?"

"Because Click doesn't need his first exposure to Christmas music to be my screeching."

"You *screech?* Cool. Let's hear it."

"Shut up, Viktor."

He chuckled just as Click reached out and touched my arm, drawing my attention his way.

"What?" I asked.

"Vee-kah."

I shook my head. "Yeah, I wish he was here, too."

But Click just frowned. "Vee-kah," he said again, and pressed his fingertips to his forehead as he closed his eyes.

"I don't understand."

He opened his golden eyes and stared at me for a moment. It was the sort of look that Floyd had used to give me when he wanted something, but I had no idea what, and he couldn't believe how clueless I was.

"Click, I—"

"Vee-kah," he said again with the familiar click, and tapped his fingers gently against his lips before pressing them to his forehead once more. I blinked rapidly, sure I was just assigning meaning where there wasn't any.

"You mean," I said slowly, choosing my words carefully, "you're talking to him in your head?"

He jerked his hand into a thumbs-up gesture so fast that I kind of startled. Then I let out a nervous laugh. His face was alight with what looked like pure happiness. Stupid Léa had finally gotten it.

"Yeah. I do that, too."

"All the time," Viktor added.

Click nodded eagerly, then touched his fingertips to my forehead. "Vee-kah."

"How did you know?" I asked, curious now about the fevered expression in his eyes. This wasn't just a matter of imagining a beloved friend. No . . . something else was going on here. "Is Viktor— Is he here right now?"

Click's expression sank into a frown, and I regretted asking the question. Disappointment swept over me. *Get a grip, Léa. Did you really want to be haunted by him? Existing in the Rift Zone is hard enough. You don't need an annoying ghost on top of everything else.*

"Hey!" Viktor said, rather indignantly. I tried to ignore him. It wasn't hard, given that Click was giving me this knowing smile. It was almost as if . . .

"You can hear me, can't you?" I whispered, my understanding starting to grow. "When I talk to him. You can hear me. Or you can sense it. Right?"

He gave me a thumbs up. My jaw dropped.

"But . . . that's not . . ."

"Possible?" Viktor offered. "Spit, Léa. You're living in a town that got torn apart by a magical pink rip in the spacetime continuum. You might need to redefine 'possible.'"

Click was waiting for me to say something else. Out loud, I figured. But I didn't really know what to say. Or do. Shaking my head slowly, I tried to form the concepts in my mind.

Poke your finger at that silver ball near the bottom of the tree, I thought, not really expecting anything to happen. But Click's eyebrows twitched a little as he seemed to listen. He turned to the tree, and my heart picked up its pace. When he extended his index finger to slowly nudge the glittery sphere, I sucked in a breath.

"Holy shit." *Do it again*, I thought. But Click just turned to me with a frown . . . until I imagined him following the command again. He turned and poked at the still-swaying ball.

"You don't understand English, do you?" I said, understanding falling into place. I looked up at Viktor, who was staring down at us with a perplexed expression. "You thought he did. But he was just reading your intention."

"Huh?"

"When you told him to do something. You probably had a picture of it in your head. He was picking up on that. Not on the words themselves."

"Huh."

"Oh, *now* you're lost for words?"

He shook his head. "Who sends someone on a student exchange when they have zero knowledge of the language of their host country?"

"Good question." I turned back to Click, who was watching the ball sway back and forth. The rough glitter caught the colourful lights, making the ornament look like it was dipped in dessert sprinkles. I turned away and looked up at the bookshelves. Grandpa had a collection of old books—though they weren't *valuable* books, so nobody had bothered to steal them. For some reason, he'd liked to collect atlases. He'd shown some of them to me, years earlier, explaining how map boundaries were constantly redrawn as new countries came into existence or were absorbed into other nations. So some of those maps were woefully out of date. There was nothing new enough to show the Rift Zone (actually, I wasn't even sure if up-to-date online maps were showing that or not), but the most recent atlas was from the early 2000s, so it would probably work for what I needed. I stood up and searched the shelves until I found the book I wanted. It was a large one, so tall that it had to be put on the shelf on its side. Pulling it out, I glanced over at Viktor. "Let's get some answers."

Click looked fascinated as I set the atlas down on the floor and opened it up. It didn't take me long to find the spread that featured Canada. The book smelled a bit musty, and when I smoothed down the pages to keep it open, a stronger waft of scent rose to my nostrils. Scanning the page, I squinted at the tiny print. Kenyonville wasn't shown, so I found the nearest major city and jabbed my finger a few millimetres away.

"We're here," I said. "Kenyonville. The Rift Zone. Or whatever they're calling it these days." I tapped the page, then touched Click's shoulder and my chest. "This is where you and I are right now."

He smiled, so I turned the pages until I found the spread with Europe.

"Show me where Reefa is."

He didn't move. When I looked at him, he was staring at the page, frowning in confusion.

"Click, where's Reefa?"

Finally, he reached out toward the atlas. But instead of pointing to any spot on the map, he started turning the pages.

"Maybe he really *is* from Australia," Viktor said. "The Great Barrier Reef?"

"He'd speak English."

"Are there islands near there? Maybe he's from one of those."

"How'd he end up in a student exchange?"

Viktor's shoulders rose in an exaggerated shrug. I turned back to Click, who had stopped turning pages. He looked to make sure I was watching, and then he jabbed his finger at the atlas. I leaned closer to have a look.

"Oh. Yeah, that's Kenyonville," I said, my voice sounding disappointed. "That's where you are now. But where did you come from? Before you came here?"

He tilted his head, his frown deepening. I was getting that "stupid Léa doesn't get it" look again.

"If he doesn't understand English," Viktor said, "you'll have to do your telepathy thing."

"It's not *my* telepathy thing," I snapped. "Besides, how do I ask him where he was living four years ago?"

"You imagine him doing an action, right?"

"Yeah. But how do I imagine him living anywhere when I don't know where that was?"

"Good point."

"And how do I imagine 'four years ago'?"

"Another good point." He reached up absently and

tightened his ponytail. "We should've looked up Reefa when we had access to the internet."

I snorted. "You were too busy checking for new followers on your social media accounts."

"Um, excuse me. I wasn't looking for new ones. I was seeing how many I'd lost."

"And how many was that?"

"Most of them." He sighed dramatically. "They think I'm dead."

"You are."

His expression fell. But not into sadness. His features just sort of went into this emotionless mask.

"Viktor?"

"Vee-kah," Click said, and, for some reason, my throat tightened. I turned to the boy sitting beside me on the floor, a boy who was watching me with a concerned expression.

"Yeah. I'm thinking about him." My voice was choked. Click reached out and wrapped his arms around me, pinning mine to my sides. I didn't have to be telepathic to know that he was probably thinking about Viktor, too.

CHAPTER 12

A SUMMONS

C-Roy's calendar just kept on going, so I knew when we crossed over into the new year, even if there was no fanfare to mark the occasion. At least, there weren't any fireworks or midnight kisses. Viktor didn't even try . . . which was just as well. The last thing I needed was to be imagining kisses with dead boys.

Click and I took down the Christmas tree on the tenth of January. Grandma had been one of those people who would put the tree up early and take it down early, often on Boxing Day. It had bothered me when I was younger. It always seemed like she was putting away the Christmas magic, stuffing it back into its boxes where it would sit for another year up in the attic. But leaving the tree up for another couple of weeks didn't feel any more special, and I was kind of glad to have the area in front of the window clear again. The living room was dim enough without an artificial tree blocking the sunlight.

We fell into a comfortable routine, and the neighbourhood stayed just static enough that I started to relax. I stuck to Joshua's territory for my raids, and I rarely ran into anyone. When I did, though, it was usually someone younger than me, and they gave me a wide berth. I wasn't sure whether to feel insulted or grateful. At twenty-one, I was smack in the middle of the Rifter demographic, though there weren't as many people around my age as there were younger teenagers thanks to the almost immediate lockdown of Kenyonville on the day of the Rift. There was no college or university in town, so those students (at least the ones who'd had classes that day) had been safely out of range. The same went for the young adults who had jobs in the next town. Kenyonville was sort of plunked in the middle of farmland and forests, a place that most people passed by (or through) but didn't really stop in. Sure, we had a decent downtown area and some swankier establishments in the south, but it wasn't like it was a place that drew a lot of tourists.

It was early March, and I was dashing through a bone-chilling sleet on my way home, a heavy backpack slung across my shoulders. I'd found the bag in one of the caches near the southern boundary of Joshua's territory about a month earlier. Someone had carelessly left it behind. But that was great news for me; I was so tired of trying to juggle heavy cans and extra-noisy packages of Cheeznudles (the supply of which seemed to be getting staler by the day . . . if such a thing was possible). Jogging down Bower Avenue, I tugged the straps forward to try to keep the load from bouncing around too much. I'd found three cans of corned beef and one can of sweet corn, and I really didn't feel like being magnanimous and leaving any of it behind. Joshua still wasn't guarding his caches very well; a few were actually heavily guarded, but since he spread the wealth out, there were a lot of hiding places that weren't guarded at all.

Which was excellent for us.

What wasn't excellent, though, was the sight that greeted me as I got closer to our house. Through the icy rain, I could just make out the two figures on the front porch. Three, if you counted the dog. A little noise of panic escaped me, a squeaky wheeze, and it took all I had in me not to sprint as fast as I could. In the Rift Zone, speed like that was likely to be seen as a threat.

"Who's that?" Viktor asked, jogging along at my side, his boots clomping on the pavement. I almost winced, fearing he would draw the stranger's attention right to us, before remembering that only I could see (or hear) him.

"This is not good," I muttered.

"Maybe the glass is half full."

"And maybe this is the day when Click and I join you."

He snorted. "If whoever that is wanted to kill Click, they would've done it already."

"Nobody wants to kill Click."

"Nobody wants to kill you, either."

I gripped the straps of the backpack tighter until the wet foam squished in my hands. Crossing the street, I slowed to a brisk walk. Click spotted me coming and pointed in my direction. "Shit," I whispered as the person standing with him turned around.

It was that kid from before. The thirteen-year-old who'd come banging on the door and given me indigestion. Shaking my head, I quickened my pace again and stormed up the front steps. I grabbed Click by the arm, spun him around, and marched him back toward the open front door.

"Buddy, come," I said to the dog who was standing on the porch, just staring at the girl. He wasn't even barking. *Some guard dog you are*, I thought.

"We're not done," the girl said as I shoved Click into the house. I stopped and turned to face her.

"Oh, yes, we are."

"No, we're not," she said, and the way she said it reminded me of a three-year-old. She held up her right hand, crossing her thumb across her palm until it touched the base of her ring finger. It was an awkward gesture, and it didn't really look like she'd had enough practice.

"What the hell is that?"

"If you'd come when you were supposed to, you would know."

"Who does your boss think he is, anyway? The school principal? Jesus Christ." I took a step backward, into the house, and grasped the edge of the door. But the girl's hand twitched, and, a moment later, I was staring at pink fire.

"Close the door," Viktor said. He was already inside, standing over by the bottom of the stairs.

"I can't," I said aloud, looking down at Buddy, who was still outside, staring up at the girl with the scarred forehead. Actually, he seemed to be staring at her glowing hand. He tilted his head.

"Yeah, you can," the girl said, and it took a moment before I realized she was answering my response to Viktor. "You're coming right now."

"Like hell. Buddy." I snapped my fingers. When that didn't pull him out of his trance, I clapped my hands. He turned, startled, and trotted into the house. I held in my sigh of relief as I started to close the door.

"Wait!" the girl said as she disappeared from view. "P-Marc said to tell you—"

"P-Marc?" I repeated, my amused disbelief overcoming my dread for a moment. Someone had obviously taken his inspiration from C-Roy . . . although, it appeared that he hadn't bothered to say the name out loud to check for any double meanings.

"Yeah, P-Marc," the girl repeated, a flicker of

confusion twisting her features. She was apparently just as oblivious as her boss. "He said to tell you to remember what happened the last time someone in this house didn't do as they were told."

My whole body froze. I desperately wanted to slam the door, run up the stairs, and hide in the attic. But that wouldn't have done much good. Especially if these people decided to take a page out of Joshua's goons' book and burn down the house with us trapped inside.

"You're all right," Viktor said, appearing at my shoulder and laying a gentle hand upon it. "Breathe, Léa."

I sucked in a slow breath and opened the door a little more so I could peer out at the girl. "You're bluffing," I said. My voice shook. I hoped she couldn't hear it.

"Do you really want to test that theory?" She shook her head. "Come on. He just wants to talk. I don't know *why*. But maybe he thinks old people are valuable or something."

"I guarantee he doesn't," I muttered, my mouth dry. I looked over at Click, who seemed awfully perplexed. That was understandable. My thoughts were a tangled mess of panic and calculation, and he was probably having a tough time reading any of them clearly.

"Look," the girl said, "it's up to you. But you're being super rude."

"Excuse me?"

"He's invited you. That's, like . . . special."

"Special," I repeated. "That's specific."

She let out a humourless grunt. "I'm just the messenger. He understands it all way better than the rest of us. And he should."

I just stared at her for a moment. "What the hell is that supposed to mean?"

"If you want to find out, I guess you'll have to do as you're told. Won't you?"

—

Arrogant little shit, I thought, for about the thousandth time, as the barely teen Rifter led me and Click deeper into P-Marc's territory. Before the Rift, this part of town had been familiar to me. Now, though, it all looked strange. And it wasn't just because of the strange markings that adorned the pavement; those had definitely not been there the previous summer when the four of us had traversed the territory. There was a weird energy that permeated the place. Some sort of end-of-the-world vibe that gave the area around the high school a whiff of decay and ozone. It felt wrong. It smelled wrong. Even the air seemed to have a weird colour tint to it, as if a filter had been pulled over the landscape. The last time we'd walked through, I'd been able to hold Viktor's hand. Now, that hand was gone, and I was too freaked out to imagine it. I thought about grabbing

Click's hand, but I didn't want to give the little bitch who was leading us any ideas. If she thought we were some sort of couple, that could've led to one of us being used as leverage. (Although, we *were* living together, so there were probably some existing assumptions about what we were to each other.)

Being homeschooled, I'd never actually set foot in the high school. After the Rift, when the military had come in and fenced off the place, I'd figured that I probably never would. The girl with the horn scars led us along the fence on the west side of the school. Just the sight of the barrier made me shudder, even though I'd seen it before. It was one of those temporary things, yellow-painted mesh panels that had been padlocked at intervals. Someone had added coils of razor wire along the top, although I didn't really know why. First, it was a school in a town full of kids. Who would want to break in? Second, the only thing of interest in there was the Rift . . . which was probably dangerous as hell. Viktor had said the government weirdos had made up that story about Cody dying after being exposed to the Rift energy. *He* had seemed to be fine (well, as fine as Viktor could've ever been), but it sounded like the kids had been whisked out of that science lab pretty quickly. If there was anything to be exposed to, it probably needed to be a prolonged exposure.

"Where are we going?" I asked, daring to pose the question that had been bouncing around my head since the girl had led us off our front porch. She glanced back at me with a dirty look. "Excuse me," I said, trying not to let my voice shake too much. "But, for all I know, you're leading us to our deaths."

She snorted. "Yeah, right. Like I'd get away with killing you before P-Marc got to have his little chat." With another glance back at us, she smirked. "But that doesn't mean I won't have fun doing it after."

She's bluffing, I thought. *The little shit is bluffing.* But I really couldn't know that for sure, and that uncertainty made my palms sweat. Even though it was still pouring rain and rivulets were dripping off the ends of my fingers, I could feel the prickle of heat. I looked down, just to make sure my hands weren't flaring.

At the back of the school, near the overflowing dumpsters (which had somehow ended up on the inside of the fence), the girl turned the corner and kept walking. Up ahead, I could see a gap in the yellow metal panels. Someone had obviously cut the lock and forced the two pieces apart by about a foot, just enough for someone to squeeze through if they turned sideways. The razor wire stretched above, but it seemed to be decorated with a strand of Christmas lights that created a sort of narrow doorway. I glanced at Click, who was staring at the very odd juxtaposition of military and twinkle. My feet scuffed to a stop on the wet, gritty path.

"Does he *live* here?" I asked. The girl, who was already through the sparkling doorway, stopped and turned back with a frown.

"What?"

"Does he live here?"

"No, he doesn't *live* here. Who'd want to live in a school?"

"I thought you were taking me to see him."

She rolled her eyes. "Yeah, dumbass. I am." Jerking her thumb over her shoulder, she shook her head. "He's in there."

"Yeah, I got that." I looked up at the building looming over us. The façade looked soaked and dark.

"You think he's going to invite strangers to his *home*? That's a great way to get murdered."

"Why? Does he have a lot of people who want to murder him?"

She shrugged. "Truth-tellers usually do."

"Truth-tellers?" I muttered as she turned around and strode toward the school. I looked at Click, who gazed back with a tired look. His denim jacket didn't have a hood, so his hair was soaked, the springy curls falling into his eyes, which looked more like bronze than gold in the dim light. "Well? What do you think?"

He tilted his head. I shook mine.

"Should we follow her in there?" I asked, trying to imagine doing so. There was a pause as he turned to gaze after the girl, who was waiting beside a still-closed door. At last, he turned back to me and gave a thumbs up. "Okay. If you're sure."

We squeezed through the glittering portal and walked up to the door, which the girl held open for us.

Even though it was pretty dark outside, what with the rain and all, it still took a few moments for my eyes to adjust to the even dimmer light inside.

"Wipe your feet," the girl said, so I scuffed my sneakers on the mat I could feel under them. A moment later, I heard Click doing the same beside me.

"Why is it so dark?" I asked, keeping my voice low so it wouldn't echo too much. Though I couldn't really see where we were, I could sense that it was some sort of hallway, judging by the way the sounds were bouncing around. "Every building in town has electricity except this one?"

A pink flare lit up the space, showing me the girl shaking her head. "Who needs electricity when we have the Rift?"

"Sorry. I wasn't aware the Rift could run a washer and dryer."

She snorted. "That's the old world. We don't need that shit."

"Is that why you stink?"

"I don't," she said, letting the insult roll off her. Probably because it wasn't true. She didn't stink. She looked pretty clean, actually. Unlike some of the feral kids in other parts of town.

She led us forward, into the darkness, her pink-glowing hand held high to light the way. When we turned a corner, I could see something up ahead. A window, maybe. It was pretty far away, though, and the light that was coming in didn't do much to illuminate the hall. What I *could* see was bathed in a pink glow. Glass cases, improbably intact, glinted on our right. They appeared to hold art projects. A time capsule from almost four years earlier, suspended and frozen for . . . well, however long they were going to keep the Rift Zone closed off from the outside world. On our left were what appeared to be bulletin boards, all holding variations of the same small poster. I squinted in the dim light, trying to read the handwritten words.

"The Children of the Rosy Dawn?" I said. "What is that? Did you guys form a band?"

The girl seemed to stiffen. But she said nothing. I swallowed and kept looking around me, wary of doorways. It was only marginally warmer inside the school, but at least it was dry. I curled my wet fingers into fists and then released them again, over and over, trying to push away the stiff chill. Firing up my pinkhands might've helped, but that probably wasn't the best idea if I didn't want to be seen as a threat.

I didn't know what I wanted to be seen as. Not weak, obviously. But beyond that . . . I wasn't sure. The situation we were walking into was an uncertain one, and I didn't have enough information to make any proper plans.

The girl turned again and led us into an echoing stairwell. But I stopped at the foot of the steps, grabbing Click's sleeve before he could follow her up to the next landing.

"Wait," I said.

"No, I'm not going to *wait*. You've been making him wait for months."

"If it was that important, he should've sent someone back sooner."

She frowned. "He has his reasons."

"Maybe he just forgot."

"Maybe. It's not for us to question."

I stared at her for a moment, my eyebrow rising in disbelief. "Who the hell do you think he is?"

"He's our *leader*," she said, as if the answer should've been obvious and she couldn't believe I was even asking the question.

"Yeah, and he's up there." I jerked my index finger upward.

"So?"

"Um . . . that's where the Rift is."

"So?"

I gaped at her. "Do you *want* to get radiation poisoning?"

"The Rift isn't dangerous."

"Right." I tilted my chin at her hand, which was still lighting up the stairwell.

"The Rift is a gift," she said, but in such a singsong way that my skin immediately started to crawl. Before I could say anything, she stepped back to the edge of the stairs and lifted her hand higher. "Follow me." The words were clipped. Not to be argued with. I had at least seven years on this kid, but something in her expression made me hesitant to disobey. We could try to run . . . but if I didn't convey the idea to Click quickly enough, he could end up with a Riftball in the back.

Hell, we both could.

I looked at him. He looked at me. With a sigh, I started up the stairs. He slipped his hand into mine. I didn't try to pull away.

I didn't know what the school had smelled like before, but I was pretty sure it was different than what it smelled like now. The ozone and decay smell was stronger. Much stronger. Sharp and sweet and apocalyptic, like death was right around the corner . . . but it was going to try to fool you into thinking everything was okay. I squeezed Click's hand, wishing for Viktor's presence at that moment. A quip. An annoying remark. A joke. Anything to take my mind off the fact that we were walking toward a tear in the very fabric of reality. The terror that built inside me felt like Rift energy, only worse. My guts churned. I felt like I needed to fart. Or cry. Or fart *and* cry, and all I wanted was for Viktor to be there to comment on *that,* and when he didn't appear, I just wanted to cry more.

At the top of the stairs, the girl led us through another doorway and into a hall that stretched off to our left. But I didn't even bother to look down it because, directly in front of us was an open doorway through which I could see something achingly bright. Something violently pink. Something that whispered with the softest hiss of plasma and what felt like existential annihilation. The girl paused. I stopped.

"Ree-fah," Click said.

CHAPTER 13

THE CHILDREN OF THE ROSY DAWN

All I could do was stand there and stare at him for a few moments as the months of questions that had been flying like frantic pigeons around my head suddenly landed in a ragged line of answers. The Rift reflected in his eyes, swirling and twisting in its pink agony, and lit up his eager expression.

Yes, it said.

Finally, it said.

Home, it said.

"Shut up," the girl whispered. "Your silent reverence is demanded."

I resisted the urge to scoff. I highly doubted the Rift demanded anything. But P-Marc was another story. *Right. P-Marc. Focus, Léa.* Click's revelation would have to wait. There were other things to worry about.

As the girl led us into the room—the science lab,

judging by the rows of lab benches that studded the space—I looked for the mysterious threat who had haunted the edges of my dreams for the last three years . . . but I was distracted by the massive pink elephant in the room.

I'd never seen the Rift. Not directly. We'd seen the eerie glow on our way back into the Zone the year before, but that was nothing compared to the sight before us. Or the smell. Or the sound. Or the sensation. All my body hair felt like it was standing on end. I shuddered involuntarily. Inexplicably. Because, as much as this thing should've been freaking me out, it wasn't. Or . . . it was trying not to. The thing felt almost conscious, and though I couldn't actually hear words, I could sense its thoughts.

You're safe.

You're all right.

Was it a trick? Some sort of predatory mechanism that it used to lure people closer, only to . . . what? Devour them? That didn't seem to be the case. There was no pull that I could feel. And the Rifters standing around the room didn't seem to be desperate to hurl themselves into the gaping pink maw, either.

There were six of them, spaced out around the perimeter of the science lab. Six sentinels, standing still, their arms raised, swirling energy cupped in their twelve hands. They all faced the Rift; I could see it reflected in a few sets of eyes. I could also see the scars, looking inflamed and angry in the pink glow that bathed the room. I looked for the girl who had led us in, but I couldn't see her. Not until she emerged from a doorway on the far side of the room. Behind her trailed an unfamiliar figure.

But I knew who he was, anyway.

Viktor had known Marc before the Rift, but he'd never told me what the guy looked like. I wondered if this person before me would've even been recognizable to those who had known him before.

He wasn't tall, but he wasn't particularly short, either. His hair swung in dark locs that fell to his shoulders, and he wore all black . . . except for what looked like a hot-pink t-shirt that peeked out from beneath his wool blazer. Most likely nineteen, he somehow had the look of someone much older. It wasn't that he had wrinkles or saggy skin or anything like that. This was something else. In the eyes. They were dark, like Viktor's. But, unlike Viktor's, these eyes felt dangerous. Even when their owner smiled.

"So," he said. "You finally decided to accept my invitation."

"It's hardly an invitation when you don't have a choice."

"You had a choice."

"Really?"

He smiled that cool smile again and waved his right hand. The girl bowed her head and scurried to the side of the room where she stood, staring at the floor. I frowned, then turned back to P-Marc, who was studying me with a skin-crawling amount of interest.

"Not what I was expecting," he murmured after way too many seconds.

"What were you expecting?"

"Someone younger. Stupider."

"Stupider?" I repeated.

He smirked. "People your age usually know what's good for them."

"Meaning . . . ?"

"Meaning, you could've been living here with us instead of raiding the little one's caches for months."

"The little one?" The laugh escaped before I could stop it. "I dare you to call him that to his face."

"Challenge accepted. If he ever ventures close enough."

"Yeah, well, he's stupid, but not stupid enough to go onto another boss's territory himself."

One side of his mouth turned up, plump lips quirking. "And what's your excuse?"

"I'm not a boss," I snapped. "I don't have to play by your rules."

He made a little hum of acknowledgement. "There's only one set of rules here."

"Yours?"

He waved his hand toward the Rift, as if that explained it all.

"That thing doesn't have rules," I said.

"Doesn't she? She gives us our gifts. There are certain ways we must use those gifts. Respectful ways."

"Mutilating your foreheads is respectful?"

He raised his eyebrows, and I noticed, for the first time, that his forehead was unmarked.

Of course it was.

"She isn't the only one who demands respect," he said softly. I wanted to take a step back, but figured that probably wouldn't be wise. So I kept my feet rooted to the floor, imagining that my soles were glued there, as he moved toward me. I could feel my eyes getting wider, and he noticed. He was enjoying this. Enjoying my fear. I wasn't sure what else I would've expected, given what he'd done to Grandpa.

"Is murder respectful?" I asked. My voice was so tight that the words came out too soft. I could barely hear myself over the hiss of the Rift and the pounding of blood in my ears. P-Marc leaned in, as if to hear better. I caught a whiff of something spicy, almost like the scent of Grandpa's deodorant.

"Murder," he said, "is sometimes necessary. But that had nothing to do with the Rosy Dawn."

I blinked. "The what?"

"Oh, I know what you call her. Again, it's about respect. How would you like to be compared to a rip? A tear? A blemish?"

I could do nothing but stand there and frown. He turned and gazed at the Rift.

"We don't use our gifts for something so . . . basic."

My fists clenched as a surge of anger washed through me. I felt the energy, stronger than I'd ever felt it before. Probably because I was standing so close to the source of that power. I had a feeling that I could fry P-Marc's face clean off in a couple of seconds if I really wanted to.

Did I want to?

"So you use guns to do the dirty work," I said. He nodded. "You know you're eventually going to run out of bullets."

"Are we?"

My heart sank. C-Roy had a supply line connected to the outside. Was it really such a leap to imagine some of the other bosses might have had one, too?

"Don't worry," he said, almost purring the words as he took another step closer. "There won't be any need for that."

"What do you want?" I asked. My voice shook. I glanced at Click, who was staring at the Rift like he'd been hypnotized. P-Marc hummed again, drawing my attention back to him.

"I want you to join your family."

"My—my family?" For a moment, I had the horrible thought that he meant Grandma and Grandpa, and my heart surged into my throat. But, as I watched his overly docile expression, I realized that wasn't what he meant. And I almost laughed. "No, thanks."

"No? Well, I'm afraid I can't allow you to continue living where you are. Those houses are for the Children of the Rosy Dawn."

"You have more houses than people. We're the only ones living on that whole block."

"Yes. In our territory."

"So?"

He shook his head. "Now, I know you're not stupid. So stop pretending you are. You have a choice to make. You can unite with your family—and enjoy all the benefits that come with such a choice—or you can find a new place to live." He tilted his head and watched the Rift for a moment. "Or, you can go back to the house you've been squatting in and expect a . . . visit."

"From you?"

He raised his eyebrows.

"With a gun, I'm guessing."

"I'm not about to waste the gifts of the Rosy Dawn on someone who doesn't even respect them. Am I?"

I didn't know what to say. This kid had obviously lost a few screws along the way . . . and gained some followers and an ego to be nourished by them. That was a dangerous combination. I swallowed hard and tried to choose my next words carefully.

"What does joining the family involve?"

He smirked. "I don't have to tell you that, do I?"

"Mutilating our faces."

"No, proudly displaying a symbol of loyalty and love to the force that changed our world for the better."

I just stared at him.

"You think I'm joking?"

"How is this *better?*" I whispered.

"How is it not? This"—he lifted both hands toward the Rift—"is pure power. This town was blessed with it. And what did all the adults—the supposed wise ones—do?"

"Ran away."

"Exactly. See? I knew you understood." He turned and rested his hands on the bench in front of him. It was probably where the teacher had once stood, back before the end of our world. "They were afraid of the Rosy Dawn. They were afraid of her gifts. But are we afraid?"

"No," six voices chorused from around the room, causing me to startle.

"No. We are loyal. We are true. We are pink."

"We are loyal," the six repeated. "We are true. We are pink."

Jesus Christ. Don't laugh. Whatever you do, Léa, don't laugh. It wasn't too hard, though. As ridiculous as the whole thing was, it was also dangerous . . . and that knowledge kept the giggles in check.

P-Marc turned back to me. He looked at Click for a moment, then returned his gaze to my face. To my forehead. "Well?"

"Can't we just pledge allegiance without messing up our faces?"

"That's not the way it works."

"What about a trade?"

He arched a skeptical eyebrow. "A trade? What could you possibly have that I'd want?"

"A truck."

The smirk oozed back onto his face. "That old thing in the garage? The battery's dead. Besides . . . where would I go?"

I didn't even want to know how he knew what he knew. Pushing the thought from my mind, I took a deep breath. But, before I could say anything, he spoke again.

"You have a decision to make."

"Why don't *you* have to have scars?"

His eyebrows rose. "Don't I?"

"Um, no. Not—" I broke off as he tugged on his sleeve, revealing his wrist. As he held it up in the pink glow of the room, I could see the dark scar that cut across the heel of his hand, almost like a tattooed bolt of lightning. It didn't look like a Riftburn.

"The kiss of the Rosy Dawn," he said, smiling fondly down at the mark. I shook my head slowly.

"What happened?"

"I was chosen."

"By whom?"

That smirk appeared again, and he let his hand fall. "Do you know how the Rosy Dawn came to grace us with her presence?"

"Yeah," I said slowly, trying to choose my words with care. "Cody's science project."

A flash of something—anger, annoyance . . . jealousy?—flashed across his features. "That's what the rest of the world thinks."

"But you know the truth?"

"*I summoned her.*"

I just stared at him and tried to keep my expression neutral. He seemed to be right on the edge of some strong emotion, and I wasn't sure I wanted to find out what that was.

"I summoned her," he repeated, more quietly this time.

"But I thought—"

"I created the spark. The Rosy Dawn came to me. She *chose* me. Why do you think she spared my life and not Cody's?"

My mind flashed and hummed with memory as I tried to recall what Viktor had told me about that day. Something about Marc messing around with the power supply on their bench. My gaze drifted over to the Rift. It was so large that it hovered over two of the smaller benches, a sweet potato-shaped blob of pink plasma that looked almost liquid, like someone had tossed a massive bucket of fruit punch into the air. I could see the power supply bulging from the surface of the bench on the right, the area around the outlets darkened as if something had caught fire and then been extinguished.

"She marked me and gave me a purpose."

"What purpose?" I asked, finally drawing my gaze away from the thing that had ruined so many lives. P-Marc's dark eyes looked glassy. He took a step closer. For a moment, I thought he might've been about to grab me by the arms to emphasize his point. But he didn't.

"To change the world."

"It already changed the world," I said. "It doesn't need you."

"We will change the world," he said, dipping his head low. His locs swung forward and his eyes narrowed. I took a step back. I couldn't help it. As soon as I did, though, he lifted his chin and the intensity seemed to fizzle. "One Child at a time," he said quietly.

"Huh?"

"Don't you see? We've been given a gift. All we have to do is accept it."

"Accept what?"

"Peace."

I coughed. "Have you not been stuck here for the last four years? What peace? That"—I pointed at the Rift—"weaponized an entire generation."

"Exactly."

"I don't understand."

"What's the best deterrent for someone with a weapon?"

I sighed as I finally got it. "Someone else with a weapon."

"Mutually assured destruction. And our generation—the beneficiaries of the gifts of the Rosy Dawn—will be the driving force."

"And just how is that going to work?"

"We break down the walls. We bring in the children. The Rosy Dawn *wants* this. The world will never again have to put up with war after war. There will be peace. And it begins with us."

There were so many things wrong with his simplistic little plan that I didn't even know where to begin. He obviously wasn't aware that the powers dissipated the farther one got from the Rift, so the only kids who would *keep* their powers would be the ones who stayed. And he seemed woefully ignorant of what really drove warfare on the planet. In his mind, it was just a matter of deterring each other with bigger and better weapons. It had nothing to do with control over people and resources.

I might as well have been talking to a five-year-old who wrote to Santa Claus to ask for world peace.

But, of course, I didn't say anything. I just nodded. He visibly relaxed.

"You understand."

"I guess," I said. I looked at Click again, wondering if he knew what was going on, what P-Marc was asking us to do. All I wanted was to grab him and make a run for it. I doubted we would get hit with any Riftballs.

Bullets, on the other hand . . .

At that thought, Click's attention snapped in my direction. I quickly shook my head, hoping to reassure him.

"So, are you ready to pledge your life to her?" P-Marc asked. He turned toward the Rift, gazing upon it like a proud parent. *Asshole*, I thought. *Even if you did create this thing, you did it by accident. And you wouldn't have been able to do it at all without Viktor's help.* I watched him stare at the pink tear in the fabric of existence like a little kid engrossed in his favourite TV show. At last, he managed to pull himself away and turn to me, eyebrows high.

"What does this pledge involve? I don't want to have to live here."

He smiled. "None of us *live* here. This is her space."

"Then . . . what?"

"We pay our respects once a month."

"Who's 'we'?"

"Her Children."

"Right." I frowned as I peered around the room. "And you all fit in here?"

"No. Only a chosen few are allowed into her chamber."

"I guess I should be honoured."

"I guess you should."

"Okay. Church once a month. What else?"

"It's not church," he said, spitting the word like it was a morsel of spoiled food. "It's a meditation on gratitude."

I wondered if P-Marc had read one too many spiritual self-help books before the Rift. Taking a deep breath, I looked over at the pink entity. "We can do that."

"The second Wednesday of every month is our sacred day. We meet here at noon."

"I don't have a watch."

"I'm sure you can figure it out from the sun." He lifted his hand and closed his eyes. My heart surged as I saw the pink flicker over his fingers. It looked a lot stronger than any Rift energy I'd ever seen before. Viktor would've had something to say about industrial-strength hand farts for sure, and I felt my chest tighten as the thought skipped around the periphery of my awareness. But he still didn't appear. Not to make snarky quips about P-Marc. Not to reassure me. And, oh, how I wanted some reassurance at that moment.

I looked at Click, trying to send him a series of mental images about what we needed to do. I didn't particularly want to feel that pain again, but I knew Click's healing touch would be able to take care of the problem. For me, anyway. I didn't know if he could heal himself, and the last thing I wanted was for him to be permanently scarred by one of my choices. He was so pretty. Almost too pretty to be real.

Are you real? I wondered as I watched him tilt his head a little, as if to listen. *Who are you?*

A little smile twitched on his lips then, and he reached up and tapped his forehead. My eyes widened.

"Are you sure?"

He gave me a thumbs up. I turned back to P-Marc, who was still standing there, his eyes closed, a schooled expression of serenity on his features. I had no idea how much of this was an act, but I suspected a good portion was. Charismatic cult leaders put on performances. And P-Marc had obviously had years to learn how to put on a good show.

"We're sure," I said, and I grabbed Click's hand. It wasn't going to make the pain any less, but at least I felt like I wasn't doing this all alone.

CHAPTER 14

THE LAYERED WORLD

y eyes watered all the way home, and I nearly tripped on Buddy as I stumbled into the foyer. I left Click to close the front door as I ran upstairs to the bathroom to check the damage. I looked awful, but it wasn't just because I had what looked like two cigarette burns pressed into my forehead. My eyes were red and puffy, my cheeks looked sunken, and my lips seemed awfully pale. Gripping the edge of the sink, I stared at my reflection for a few moments, listening to the sounds of the old house . . . and then Click's footsteps as he bounded up the stairs. I turned in time to see him almost bounce into the bathroom, his skirt swinging over his jeans. He walked right up to me and raised his hand to my forehead, letting his fingers hover over the skin. I didn't have the energy to argue.

"I'm so sorry," I said as my gaze fixed on the

identical marks that he now wore. "I just didn't know of any other way to get him to leave us alone."

He smiled a little, but didn't make any other movements. I could already feel that soft energy coursing over my skin like warm, soothing water. The two marks on my forehead tingled, and I knew the skin was already healing. Regenerating.

"You're . . . not human."

His smile broadened for a moment, like he'd understood me perfectly but found my conclusion pretty damn amusing. Lifting his other hand, he placed the fingers gently over my heart. "Lee-ah," he said, the click at the end so soft I almost didn't catch it. "Ah-ee." He moved his fingers to his own heart.

"We're not the same. You're . . . You can heal people. I can't. It's not something we—"

"Ree-fah."

"Yeah, I know. I still don't know how that happened. But—"

"Ree-fah," he said again. His hand—the one hovering over my forehead—came to rest gently against my skin. I braced myself, thinking for sure that it was going to hurt like hell. But it didn't. I frowned.

"You can't be done yet," I said, pulling back and turning to the mirror. I blinked. The marks were gone. Well, not *gone*. I could see the new, pinkish skin, and a few flakes of the old, damaged tissue were still tenaciously clinging. I rubbed them away, carefully, my eyes wide. "Holy shit."

"Ree-fah."

My mind whirled as I tried to understand what he was saying. I turned back to him, shaking my head. "The Rift? You can do this because of the Rift?"

He tilted his head a little, a frown of confusion creasing his features. Finally, he reached for my hand. "Lee-ah," he said, pulling my hand up to hover over his forehead.

"Click, I can't—"

"Ree-fah," he said, and closed his eyes. He took a deep breath. He let it out with a soft hum, the way he'd done when he'd healed the mark from Rasputin's thumb.

Oh, what the hell? I thought. *I might as well try. It's not going to make things worse.* So I took a deep breath and tried to mimic the hum. Then I imagined healing energy running through me, all the way from my heart, down my arm, and into my hand. My fingers grew warm, and a twinge of panic distracted me for a moment as I worried that I was about to send Rift energy directly onto his already-damaged skin. But there was no glow. There was just that soft, warm feeling, like my hand was encased in a plush puppet.

He held my wrist there for so long that my shoulder started to ache, and I felt despair sink over me. It wasn't working. And I'd gone and made him scar his pretty face to appease some weird-ass teenage cult leader. Some friend I was.

"Click," I whispered, my arm beginning to shake. Slowly, he opened his golden eyes and let go of me. I pulled my hand away, not wanting to see the mess I'd made (or, rather, the mess I hadn't been able to clear up). So when I saw the two shiny patches on his golden skin, I nearly peed my pants. "No."

He gave me a thumbs up. All I could do was stare at him. And shake my head.

"I . . . can't."

"Ree-fah," he said, his face lit up in a knowing grin. "Lee-ah." He reached up and rubbed at the healed marks, brushing away the dead blister bits.

"The Rift *heals* people?"

He shook his head. "Lee-ah."

"But I'm not—" I broke off as I understood. "The Rift helps *us* heal people."

A long moment passed as he seemed to be listening to my thoughts. I had so many questions, and this was a painstaking way of getting information. Remembering the stacks of stuff in the attic, I pushed past him, nearly tripped on Buddy again, and headed for the ladder.

"Take him outside," I said as I disappeared up into the musty, dusty space. "He's probably busting. And then meet me down in the living room."

—

I wasn't sure why I'd decided to store my stationery in the attic, but I was glad I had. Aside from some gel pens that had dried up, most of the writing implements—markers, coloured pencils, and ballpoint pens—were working fine. There was even half a ream of printer paper (of course, the printer was long gone), so that got hauled downstairs as well. I arranged everything on the floor where the Christmas tree had stood, wondering if my plan was going to work. When I heard the front door open and close a few minutes later, I looked up to find Click staring at the stationery with a contemplative expression on his face. Buddy trotted right into the living room and gave everything a good sniff. I grabbed him and pulled him out of the way.

"Come sit down," I said, setting the dog beside me where he obediently plunked his butt on the floor. Click smiled and walked closer, still staring at the objects I'd arranged. He lowered himself gracefully, tucking his feet under his knees. "Can you tell me about your home?"

His eyes seemed to light up. "Ree-fah," he said, pointing toward the back of the house. North. Toward the school.

"Yeah. You came through the Rift. Obviously. But where are you from? What's it called?"

He seemed to be listening. When I was done speaking, though, his expression sank into a frown. "Ree-fah," he said slowly.

"That's what you call the Rift. Your language only has, like, two vowel sounds." I watched him for a moment. "You probably don't use spoken language much, though, do you? You don't need to."

"Ree-fah," he repeated, jabbing his finger north again.

I shook my head and placed my hand on my chest. "I'm Léa. I live in Kenyonville." I waved my hands to indicate the space around us. "And you . . ."

"Ah-ee," he said, adding the click at the end. "Ree-fah."

This was going nowhere, fast. I tried to think of a way to explain it when he spoke again.

"Lee-ah. Kah-nah."

I waited for him to finish the word, but he didn't. "Kenyonville."

"Kah-nah."

"Two vowel sounds, and no words with more than two syllables. Got it."

He smiled. "Lee-ah. Kah-nah," he said, pointing at me. "Ah-ee. Ree-fah." He pointed at his chest. A slow frown spread across my face as a thought occurred to me.

"Reefa? The place where you're from is actually called Reefa?"

The double thumbs up came so fast that I couldn't stop the laugh that burst out of me.

"So it's just a coincidence that you say 'Rift' and 'Reefa' the same way?"

"Ree-fah."

"Okay. Got it." I paused. "What do you call the Rift in your language?"

He shook his head and tapped his lips.

"There's no word for it?" I guessed. "Or . . ." He sat

patiently, waiting for me to figure something out. "Do you even use words? Besides for proper names?"

In response, he tapped his lips and pointed at himself. He tapped his lips and pointed at Buddy. He tapped his lips and pointed at me. He tapped his lips and pointed north.

"How do you store information?" I asked. "I mean . . . without language. You don't have books, do you?"

His gaze travelled up to the bookcase for a moment. He frowned.

"So . . . how?"

He reached for one of the coloured pencils—the hot pink one—and leaned over the stack of paper. *Finally,* I thought. But I wasn't prepared for what I saw. He held the pencil strangely, though not awkwardly, as he quickly sketched out a scene on the page. There were two simple figures, one slightly taller than the other. Both wore what looked like knee-length skirts.

"Is that you?" I asked, pointing to the shorter one. He smiled and continued sketching. I leaned closer, in awe of the sureness of his movements. He looked like he'd been doing this for years. "You might not have written language . . . but you have art, don't you?" Joining the drawings already on the page was a chaotic, elongated shape with jagged edges that hovered over the heads of the two figures. "The Rift?" I asked.

"Ree-fah." But he didn't stop there, and proceeded to sketch a tall triangle that pointed upward, touching one end of the Rift. He followed that up with a second . . . whatever it was.

"Are those towers?" Shaking my head, I leaned closer. They weren't large enough to be actual towers, unless the respective sizes were way off. And I doubted they were. He paused in his sketching to point at the Rift on the page.

"Ree-fah."

"Yeah. I get that."

He thought for a moment, then turned back to the page and poked the tip of the pencil at the shorter figure's head. Twice.

"The burns that P-Marc gave us?"

He tapped the pencil against the Rift.

"The Rift helps people heal things," I said slowly, trying to figure out what he was attempting to say. "But . . . I don't understand what the pointy things are."

"Ree-fah."

I sighed, deciding to try a different approach. "Who's that?" I asked, pointing to the taller figure. "Your father?"

He frowned. "Kah-nee," he said, punctuating the word with a click.

"Connie?"

"Kah-nee," he said slowly, like I was an idiot.

"Hey, you can't say my name properly, either." I looked at the person on the page. "Not your father. Your . . . mother?"

He sighed, seemingly troubled by his lack of

words. Really, though, he was probably just frustrated by me and my non-telepathic ass.

"Your boss?" I asked. He tilted his head, his eyebrows raised a little. I felt like I was getting close. "Your teacher?"

He gave me a thumbs up.

"Okay. Connie the teacher. What were they teaching you?"

The pencil tip tapped the illustrated Click's forehead again.

"Healing? And . . . the Rift was helping?"

Another thumbs up. I peered at the drawing with a frown.

"So the Rift was there. In your world. And it helps you heal people . . ." Trailing off, my gaze snapped to the triangles. "Oh, my god. It's a machine, isn't it? Or a device. A healing device. Towers with energy—the Rift—zapping between them."

Click dropped the pencil so he could give me two thumbs ups at once. I laughed.

"You guys must be way more advanced than us. A bunch of telepathic healers. And you got stuck in this shithole with a bunch of idiots who can't stop trying to kill each other."

He frowned. "Lee-ah. Vee-kah."

"We're the exceptions."

Glancing at Buddy, who had decided to take a nap on the floor beside me, he smiled. Then he picked up the pencil again. I wasn't sure what else he was going to draw, what else he was going to blow my mind with. But he set that piece of paper aside and leaned over a new one. This time, he drew three figures: a very tall one on the left, a shorter one in the middle, and something small and obviously not human on the right. It took me a moment to realize what that thing was.

"Buddy?" I asked, pointing to the stylized creature. Click kept drawing, adding a few more details. None of the figures had facial features, but on the tall one, he started to draw some. One eye. A scribble down one cheek. "Viktor," I said. "And me."

"Vee-kah. Lee-ah. Bah-dee."

"Nice."

He dropped the pencil and reached for the paper he'd set aside. I frowned, not sure what he was doing as he took the new drawing, placed it on top of the old one, and held both up to the dim light coming in the window. Through the paper, I could see the faint outlines of the original drawing of the two figures and the Rift device. He looked at me expectantly.

"Um . . . I don't get it."

Undeterred, he set the papers down again and returned to the original. Pointing his finger at the illustrated Click, he checked to make sure I was looking. "Ah-ee."

"Yeah. That's you."

He moved his finger up, sharply, toward the Rift while he made a little sucking noise with his mouth.

He grabbed the second drawing, set it on top again, and poked his finger at the same area, repeating the sound. Then he took up the pencil and started to sketch again, adding a third human figure beside the dog.

"Holy shit," I breathed. "The Rift sucked you up in your world . . . and spat you out here?"

He gave me a thumbs up with his free hand.

"But how? Does this happen often?"

He frowned.

"I didn't think so." I chewed on my lip as I tried to recall everything I'd ever been told about the Rift. And my mind could only come up with one thing. "It was the power supply in the science lab. Whatever Marc did that day. It must've interacted with Viktor's science project." My eyes widened. "Oh, my god. Viktor's science project."

Click just stared at me. I wasn't sure what to do to make him understand what I was thinking. I didn't even know what Viktor's device had looked like. All I knew was what it was for. "He said it was something to do with healing. Was it like your device? Is that why . . . Did that spark from the power supply create some sort of wormhole between the two devices? Between our two worlds?" Moving aside the top piece of paper, I pointed to the Rift that Click had sketched on the one underneath. His features relaxed a little, and I knew he'd understood what I was trying to ask.

"Ree-fah," he said, slipping the second paper over

the first and pressing his finger on the vague image of the Rift that we could see bleeding through.

"No shit." I shook my head, my mind reeling. "So . . . are your people looking for you? Is that why the Rift is still there? They left the device running? Or . . ." Trailing off, I watched as he held his arms out to the sides, his palms facing up. Slowly, he lowered one hand while raising the other. Then he reversed the motion. "Balance?" I guessed.

He pointed to the image of himself on the second paper. The Click in *our* world.

"You're not supposed to be here," I said slowly. "So . . . there's no balance."

He smiled, an eager expression in his eyes. I must've been close to finally getting it.

"Shit," I whispered. "You being here . . . Is that what's holding the Rift open?"

The two big thumbs ups made my heart surge. I just stared at him, trying to make sense of the implications.

"So if you go through it again . . . If you go home . . ." Shaking my head, I listened to the words in my own mind. *The Rift will close. This will all be over.*

"Lee-ah," he said, the words jolting me back to the present, away from the strange hope that had started to bubble within me.

"Yeah?"

"Vee-kah."

"It's too late for Viktor," I said, my throat tightening

on the words. Click frowned. He looked at his drawings again, then back at me. "But it's not too late for you, is it?"

He reached out and took my hand. I gave it a quick squeeze.

"It's time for you to go home, Aï," I said, doing my best with the click at the end of the name. He looked like he wanted to laugh . . . but he seemed pleased that I'd at least given it a shot.

CHAPTER 15

CLOSED

There was no time to waste. The Children of the Rosy Dawn were having their cult meeting (service? I had no idea what to call it) in less than 24 hours. We had to get the Rift closed before then . . . not least because I didn't know how I was going to explain my unmarked forehead.

"Please let this work," I muttered to myself as I peered out the open back door to where Click was gallivanting with Buddy as the sun rapidly descended toward the horizon. They were playing some game in which Click would pretend to throw a stick, and Buddy would go chasing after it before realizing nothing had been thrown. The dog kept falling for it, though, so many times that I wondered if Click was using some sort of telepathic trick that animals could pick up on.

"It will," Viktor said, suddenly at my left shoulder.

I startled a little, edged to the side, and looked up at him. He stared out the door, a serene expression on his face as he watched the boy and his dog play in the deepening twilight.

"You don't know that."

"How do you know?"

"Because *I* don't know that. And you're just a figment of my imagination."

He turned and looked down at me with a smile, the expression twisting the lumpy scar on his cheek. "Daydreaming about me, are you?"

"Shut up." My voice sounded tired. And sad. I watched Click and Buddy for a few more seconds, then took a deep breath. "I need you to do something for me."

"What's that?"

"I need you—"

"Yeah . . ."

"—to stop visiting me."

"No . . ."

"Viktor."

"Léa. I'm not going to do that."

I turned to him, scowling. "Even if this is what I need?"

"You need me."

"No, I don't. And I . . . can't."

"You can't?" he said, his eyebrows rising.

"Can't do this anymore. Can't remember you anymore. It's too hard. And once Click's gone..."

"You'll need me more than ever."

"No!" I said, the word almost a shout. "It'll be too hard."

"Why?" His voice was soft. Gentle. So much like the sweet kid that I knew he could be.

"Because it won't be real. And I'll know it won't be real." My eyes swam as I tried to blink back the tears. "When I'm here on my own, I'll need to . . . move on."

He frowned. "You're not going to leave?"

My shoulders lifted in a shrug. "I don't know yet," I admitted. "I haven't thought that far ahead."

"What's there to think about? Do you really want to stay in this heckhole?"

"I might not have a choice." I shook my head and turned to look out the door again. "I thought there were only two options: One, nothing happens. Click can't get home. The Rift stays open. And we'll just have to adapt."

"Okay."

"Two, it works. Click goes home. Balance is restored to the universe. The Rift closes. And the walls will come down."

"My money's on that one."

"You're dead. You don't get a vote."

He grunted in amusement. "Was there another option?"

"Yeah. Three, it half works. Click goes home, but the Rift doesn't close. The Zone will stay locked up. And I'll be stuck in here, alone."

"You won't be. You'll have me."

"Just what I want. An invisible guy to snark at until I get a reputation as the batshit bitch of Bower Avenue."

He shook his head. "You wouldn't stay here, would you?"

"I don't know." With a sigh, I let my gaze drift to what I could see of the school. "I'm tired, Viktor. Fighting just doesn't seem worth it anymore."

"So you're going to let Permanent Marc redo your devil bites so you can kiss his ass on the second Wednesday of every month? I don't know, Léa. That sounds like a pretty stupid plan to me."

"Well, like I said, you're dead. You don't get a vote."

"If you're going to give up, why not give up in C-Roy's territory?"

"I'm trying to forget you," I said, stepping away from him and out the door. "And I can't do that in the place where I lost you."

He didn't say anything. I turned back to look, and he was gone.

Gone gone.

I could feel it. And though it hurt—knowing I wouldn't see him again felt like a hot weight in the middle of my chest—the feeling was also a bit of a relief.

In our world, sometimes we needed to block out certain emotions if we wanted to survive.

—

didn't think about a flashlight until we were halfway to the school, and by then it was too late to go back and look for one. Besides, I didn't know if Grandpa's old one was still in the house or if it had been pilfered at some point while I'd been away.

It's fine, I told myself. *If Click goes through and the Rift closes, you'll just have to wait until morning before you leave. No big deal. The Children of the Rosy Dawn aren't having their service until noon. You'll have plenty of time to get out of the school before then.*

Buddy trotted along just ahead of us, looking back every so often to make sure Click was still following. It was like he knew there was a big goodbye coming up. I hadn't had the heart to tell Click the dog had to stay home; I remembered how hard it had been for him to leave Buddy with Dr. Bryan when we'd left the Zone the previous year. They only had a little time left with each other, and I wasn't going to stand in the way of that.

The sky had finally cleared—mostly—so the moon shone overhead, only occasionally blotted out by clouds. There was no need for pinkhands at all; we could see well enough. The streets were quiet. Too quiet. I had the feeling that people were watching us from the shadows, peeking out from behind curtains. Still, nobody came to confront us, and by the time we reached the fence at the front of the school, I was starting to relax a little, even though the eerie pink glow that oozed through the windows should've been making me freak out.

In silent agreement, we hugged the fence as we made our way around the side to the back of the school. Even Buddy seemed to know where we were going. He sniffed his way along the base of the fence, engrossed as if a hundred other dogs had lifted their legs there. It wasn't likely; I hadn't seen any other dogs for years. A few cats that had managed to survive that awful first winter, sure. But dogs were about as rare as mature adults in Kenyonville.

Probably more rare.

By the time we reached the gap in the fence, Buddy had fallen to the back of our pack. I snapped my fingers at him, but when that didn't work, I poked Click with my finger and thought about what I wanted him to do. After a couple of seconds, he bent down and scooped the dog into his arms. Buddy didn't complain; he just sort of wrapped his front paws around Click's forearm like he always did.

The string of twinkle lights glowed steadily in the cold night air. We ducked through the gap, causing the lights to wobble and the shadows to sway. Only when we were safely on the other side did I notice the problem.

"Shit," I whispered, staring at the figure who lounged on a ragged lawn chair beside the back door to the school. *Shit, shit, shit,* my mind continued. The person had seen us. They leaned forward, peering into the darkness. Click and I exchanged a look.

"You lost?" The voice was deep and masculine. A

moment later, the figure unfolded itself from the chair, and my heart sank a little more. He was *huge*. But that didn't deter Click, who walked forward, clutching Buddy against his chest.

"Fuck," I whispered, drawing the word out as I scurried after them. "Click, let's go."

But he didn't seem to have heard me. Either that, or he didn't care. Could I really blame him? He'd been stuck in the Rift Zone for the last four years, separated from his family and friends. His teacher, too. Being so close to that interdimensional portal must've been almost more than he could bear. It was probably like standing right next to a subway gate and not having any money for the fare.

"Hey, kid," the big guy said. "You want to turn around and walk away before anyone gets hurt?"

"Sorry," I said, my voice coming out breathy and tight. "He . . . doesn't understand."

Click turned and gave me a quizzical look. *Just go with it*, I thought, then realized he probably couldn't decipher that sort of command very well.

"He stupid or something?"

"No," I said, bristling. "He's super smart. But he's an exchange student. His English still isn't very good."

The guy let out a low whistle. "Sucks to be him."

"Yeah. No kidding." I tried to force out a laugh. Maybe, if we acted casual enough—

"Where'd you find a dog?"

"In some dead guy's house."

"Yeah?"

"Yeah. The dog actually ate the guy's face, so . . . you probably don't want to make any sudden, threatening moves."

The big guy didn't say anything for a few moments. He was looking at Buddy, though, probably wondering how a scruffy little thing who was, at that moment, clinging to Click's arm like a lost child could've eaten someone's face.

"Does P-Marc know you have that thing?" he asked at last.

"I was under the impression that he knew pretty much everything."

He grunted. "Sure."

I didn't know what to make of that response. Were things not quite as black-and-white as P-Marc had attempted to make them look? Peering into the shadows, I tried to see the guy's forehead. But he was wearing a dark toque, and it was pulled down rather low.

"Look," I said, tired of standing there, getting colder and more nervous as the seconds ticked by. What did I have to lose? "We just came to pay our respects."

"Your respects?" the guy repeated. "To P-Marc?"

"No. To the Rosy Dawn."

"You're a few hours early."

"Yeah, I know. But . . . it's not the same. You know?"

"Not the same," he repeated.

"Yeah. With all those people there. It should be a sacred experience. Intimate."

I could see his eyebrows rise, even with the hat. "You one of those weirdos that gets off on the pink?"

"What? No." I frowned. *How the hell does* that *work?* I wondered, then decided I probably didn't want to know the details. "We just want a few minutes alone with her. Without all the ceremony."

He didn't say anything for so long that I thought for sure he was going to tell us to leave. And then he'd go straight to P-Marc and tell him all about the weird nocturnal visitors to his precious Rosy Dawn.

And then we'd be royally screwed.

But the guy just sighed, settled his toque a little more firmly on his head, and waved one hand at the door as he went back to his lawn chair. "Knock yourselves out."

"Really?" I said, which made him pause in a sort of crouch, his butt halfway to the chair.

"Yeah, really." He sat down the rest of the way and stretched his legs out in front of him. *God. They must have plenty of food in this part of town. How does a Rifter even get that big?* "Door's unlocked," he said. "As usual."

Click didn't waste any time. He scurried to the door, still holding Buddy. I followed a little more slowly, keeping a wary eye on the big guy in the chair. Was this some sort of trap? *You've got Rifthands,* I reminded myself. But then, on the heels of that, came another thought. *They've got Rifthands and guns.*

I almost stopped. But Click was already waiting at the door, his arms full of dog and his face full of hope, and I couldn't begrudge him his chance. I didn't know when he might get another one. So I forced myself to keep walking, grabbed the cold metal handle, and hauled the door open.

I could hear Click wiping his feet, which almost made me laugh. But I didn't really feel like laughing. The smell of the Rift was overpowering inside the school, and it really made my skin crawl. The hallway was even darker than it had been the first time we'd been in it, so I lifted my right hand and pushed some glow through to my fingertips. My body flinched as the shadows shifted and shiny objects—door handles, windows, the glass cases along the walls—threw reflections back at us. For a moment, I thought I saw eyes. I stepped forward with a shudder.

"Let's go," I whispered. "Stay close. It's really dark in here."

Click stayed at my elbow as we made our way toward the stairwell that led up to the second floor. Before we even reached the top, I could detect a faint pink glow permeating the air above us, almost like a mist. Our feet sounded overly loud on the steps, and I held my breath as we climbed, listening for voices. I couldn't hear any, but that didn't necessarily mean much. If there were any cult members in the science lab, standing there in silent contemplation . . .

Click deposited Buddy at the top of the stairs, and the

dog trotted off before I could say anything. We followed, because of course he headed right into the classroom where the Rift hung, suspended, over the science benches. In the darkness of night, with nothing but a bit of moonlight streaming in through the windows, the Rift was hard to look at, so bright it hurt my eyes. It still looked pink, though, despite how intense it seemed; I would've expected it to look white. Buddy approached slowly, then stopped when he was between the two benches, tipping his nose up to give the Rift a good sniff.

"Are you *sure* you came through that?" I asked. Click turned to me, eyebrows raised. The room was so bright, I could see him clearly. I quickly shook away the pink energy I'd forgotten I was holding. "It looks dangerous."

"Ree-fah," he said, reaching up to trace his fingers over my cheekbone, my jaw, and then my forehead.

"Yeah, it helped heal us. But . . . it's powerful. And if it's strong enough to create a portal between parallel universes, do you really want to—" I broke off. "Wait. What *are* you going to do?"

He turned and looked at the pink rip of energy. It hovered in place a few feet above the benches. Buddy stood up on his hind legs, still sniffing. He seemed pretty calm, considering what loomed above him.

Click moved into the room, closer to the Rift. My hand shot out, my fingers closing around his wrist.

"Wait."

"Lee-ah," he said, his voice gentle as he removed

my hand from his arm. My heart started to pound, and a crushing sense of despair swept over me.

What is wrong with you? This is what should've happened years ago. If you were the one trapped in another world, wouldn't you be more than ready to go home? Curling my fingers into fists, I took a step back, staring at the floor. I thought Click would start moving toward the Rift again, but he didn't. I could see his sandal-clad feet just standing there. I wasn't surprised when those feet moved toward me, and I found myself enveloped in a hug.

I started to cry. It was such a rare thing for me, and yet it felt so familiar. All I could remember was the last time I'd had to say goodbye. It shouldn't have mattered. A year earlier, before I'd met my friends, I'd been alone. Surrounded by other Rifters, yes . . . but cut off from any sort of friendship. Or love. I curled my fingers into Click's jacket, pulling at the stiff denim as I clung to him.

"Vee-kah," he said as he pulled away. I shook my head and wiped my wrist under my dripping nose.

"I can't think about him. It hurts too much."

He frowned.

"It's okay," I said. "I'll manage. I've been on my own before. I can do it again." I reached out and laid one hand on his cheek. "I'm going to miss you, Aï."

He gave me a little nod, his golden eyes glowing pink in the reflections from the Rift. Though he might not have understood my words, I knew he understood what I meant.

He took a step away and shrugged out of his jacket. It fell to the floor as he bent down to unfasten his sandals. The ratty socks followed, much to Buddy's delight; he grabbed one and trotted away with it, as if he expected Click to go chasing after him. But Click didn't seem to notice. He peeled off the jeans from under his skirt, then slipped his sandals back on. For the first time, I saw him as he really was: a stranger trapped in an even stranger land. His beaded blouse, pleated skirt, and strappy sandals suddenly made perfect sense, and I understood why he'd always resisted taking them off. They were a part of his world. A reminder of home.

"Bah-dee," he called softly, turning away from me to search the pink-drenched science lab for the wayward dog. Buddy peeked out from behind a bench on the far side of the room, the sock still dangling from his mouth. Click crouched down, not saying a word. But the dog dropped the sock, licked his own nose, and walked over to his best friend. Click gathered him into his arms, bowing his curly head so he could press his face into the scruffy white fur. Buddy rested there, patiently, almost as if he were listening. He probably was.

Whatever Click had to say to the dog took a while. When he was done, he kissed the top of Buddy's head and set him on the floor. Standing up, he turned to me.

"Ree-fah," he said.

"I know."

He gave me a little smile, then looked up at the Rift as it shimmered and whispered above the science lab.

"How are you going to do this?" I asked. He looked around, then strode to the teacher's bench at the front of the room. I hurried after him, my heart in my throat as he clambered up, and tried not to stare up his skirt. (I knew enough about Click's people to know they didn't do underwear.) Buddy trotted up to me and scratched at my ankle with a whine. But I ignored him, focusing instead on the boy standing above me, facing the Rift. I knew he was going to jump. I knew he had to. A part of me hoped it would work.

A part of me hoped it wouldn't.

He turned back to me, and I looked up, seeing him silhouetted like a pink angel. He lifted his hand to his chest. "Lee-ah," he said. "Vee-kah."

I didn't bother to correct him. "Yeah. We're going to miss you. We love you, Aï."

He closed his eyes as he tapped his chest—his heart—as if to say, "I love you, too." And then he turned. He took a step.

And he jumped.

I wasn't sure what I expected to happen. An explosion of light, maybe. But what happened in the next instant was the opposite. As Click's body hit the Rift, it seemed to create a vacuum. My hair swung forward, pulled by the suction. Weirder than that, though, was the way all the light in our world seemed to suck into that space with such force that it felt like my eyeballs were going to be pulled right out of my head. But before I could even close my eyes, it was over. The background hiss, like what I remembered hearing at the end of one of Grandpa's old LPs, was suddenly gone, and all I could hear were Buddy's nails on the floor. My eyes, still accustomed to the brilliance of the Rift, watered as they tried to adjust to the darkness. To the emptiness of the science lab.

"It's over?" I whispered. It didn't seem possible. And yet, the Rift was gone. Click was gone. I hadn't heard his body hit the benches, and I surely would have if the portal hadn't swallowed him. Leaning my hands on the cool edge of the teacher's bench, I peered into the darkness, waiting for the sparkling to dissipate. My eyes slowly readjusted, and the room came back into focus. I could see the lab benches, lit now only by the feeble moonlight. The ones below where the Rift had sat for four years—four years of pain, fear, loneliness, and abandonment—were empty. "It's over," I said. This time, it wasn't a question.

Buddy let out a little whine. I turned to look down toward the noise, but couldn't see anything in the shadow of the teacher's bench. Automatically, I raised my hand, trying to push the familiar energy into my fingers. Nothing happened. A small pang of regret tweaked my chest, but then it was gone.

"Come here," I said, carefully sitting down on the floor behind the bench. I held one hand out, hoping Buddy would come closer so I could touch him. I felt his little sniffs first. Then a cold nose. And then a warm tongue. "I know. You wanted to go with him. But that probably would've upset the balance the other way." He moved closer, and I managed to work my fingers into the scruffy hair around his ears. "He loved you, though. A lot. You'll have to settle for me now."

He let out a sound like a disgusted sneeze, then wandered away. I didn't really feel like chasing after him in the dark school. But I doubted he would go far; he seemed to like to stay close to humans. Losing his original pet parent in such a traumatic way might've had something to do with that.

I debated turning on the lights so I could see enough to make my way outside, but decided I didn't really want to risk it. There would be plenty of time to leave in the morning. Early, so I wouldn't run into the Children of the Rosy Dawn.

I sucked in a breath. *What are they going to do when they find the Rift gone?* That was something I hadn't really considered. P-Marc was not going to be happy. And if he found me here . . .

Did I really have a choice? The school was pitch black. If I turned on any lights, I would give myself away to anyone who might've been watching the building. If I tried to make it back to the exit in the dark, I could end up falling down the stairs and damaging myself. And with Click gone, I would be looking at a painfully normal—and potentially long—recovery.

I decided to go with what seemed like the least

terrible of my options, scooting back until I could lean against the wall. The room grew cool—apparently, the Rift had been providing a bit of heat—so I zipped my jacket all the way up and shoved my hands into my pockets where they encountered two paper objects. I didn't need light to know what they were: the photo of my family and the wrinkled exit pass from Dr. Frazier. One was a reminder of something I didn't want to forget. The other was a reminder of something I wished had never happened.

But I didn't want to give up either one.

I closed my eyes and leaned my head back, suddenly so weary. I didn't know what time it was, but on any other night I probably would've been curled up in bed, fast asleep. I longed for that bed now, even though I would probably have to share it with a dog going forward. *There are worse things*, I thought as I felt myself drift and tilt toward sleep. Random images danced around my mind as slumber approached. I tried to ignore the hard floor. The cold room. The empty darkness.

"Léa?" Viktor whispered. I was just conscious enough to be annoyed as I wrapped my arms around myself and turned my head away, still keeping my eyes tightly shut.

"Go away." I spoke the words out loud. What did it matter now? "You're not supposed to be here."

I heard his footsteps on the floor as he walked closer, and then a gentle hand settled on my shoulder. I jerked.

"Can't you *ever* do what I ask?" The words sounded miserable. "I just need you to go."

"Why?"

"Because I'm going to lose my mind. I've probably already lost it. And you being here isn't helping."

"I'm sorry."

"I have to move on. I have to do this on my own. I'm probably going to mess it up and get myself killed, but—"

"Who's going to kill you?"

I sighed. "It doesn't matter."

"I'd say it does."

"You would."

He made what sounded like the tiniest laugh, just a little huff of air.

"Please, Viktor."

"I'm not going anywhere, Léa. You'll just have to put up with me."

I slumped against the wall, feeling like I wanted to cry. Even the imaginary Viktor was enough to frustrate me to tears.

But a part of me was glad that, as much as I consciously protested, my mind was going to keep inflicting him on me. At least for now.

CHAPTER 16

THE EXQUISITE PAIN

My ass hurt. My legs also seemed to be partially asleep. But the right side of my body was oddly comfortable. And warm. I swam out of a half-finished dream that I couldn't remember, confused for a moment. *Where the hell am I?* I thought, just as my eyes focused on the cupboards of the bench in front of me. I blinked a few times, lifting my head from—

"Fuck!" I said, my body spurting to its feet as I registered the fact that I wasn't alone. And I wasn't talking about the dog. Adrenaline coursed through my body, down into my empty-feeling hands. No Rift energy. That was going to take some getting used to. But that acclimation would have to wait until I wasn't stuck in a science lab with a strange—

"Spit, Léa. Stop."

I was almost out the door on the far side of the room

(even though I had no idea where it led), but the words—the voice—stopped me. Bracing my hands on the doorframe, I closed my eyes and tried not to let my knees buckle. "This is not good," I muttered.

"What's not good?"

"This." I bowed my head. "I knew my brain would explode sooner or later."

There was a little grunt, and then footsteps coming closer. I sucked in a breath and backed away, prepared to face down this hallucination, even if he wouldn't do as I asked. But as I opened my eyes and looked up, my body let out an involuntary squeak. It wasn't Viktor after all, and I had to keep my feet still as they longed to sprint out the doorway, away from the strange guy standing a few feet away in the dawn-lit science lab. He was tall (like Viktor) and skinny (like Viktor), but there were differences, too. The way he walked, for one thing, halting and uneven. His dark hair was cut short and neat, styled with great care with what looked like a decent amount of product. *Where did he get that in the Zone?* I wondered numbly as I watched him approach. I wasn't sure I wanted to look up into his face, but I did, noting the dark eyes behind a pair of stylishly nerdy glasses. I took another step back, and he stopped his advance.

"Who are you?" I whispered. A small, uncertain smile twitched on his mouth.

"Who am I?"

"I asked you a question. Don't just repeat it back to me. Who the hell are you?" My fingers twitched as I tried—ineffectually—to drive some Rift energy into them. The guy frowned.

"Léa . . ."

"How do you know my name? Did P-Marc send you?" My hands found the doorframe again as I took a step backward. I had to get out of there. P-Marc probably knew about the Rift, that Click had destroyed his precious Rosy Dawn. But I was the only one still in the school, so the blame was going to fall squarely on my shoulders. "Show me your hands!" I shouted. The guy lifted them, looking startled. "Do you have a gun?"

"What? No, Léa . . . I'm sorry. I don't know what's going on here, but—"

"Who are you?" I shouted.

"You know who I am."

I shook my head. "Don't mess with me." My hands curled into fists, and I brought them up to my head, rapping them against my skull as if I were knocking on a door. "Please. Leave me alone. Leave me alone!"

He strode forward and grabbed my wrists, shattering any last illusion that he was just a figment of my imagination. His hands were strong, and they were warm, and they were very, very real.

"Who are you?" I asked again, straining at his grip, trying not to break into sobs.

"I'm Viktor," he said, his voice tipping into a tone

that made me think he was talking down a wild animal.

I shook my head. "He's dead." I wrenched hard, but he wouldn't let go. "He's dead!" I screamed. "He walked in front of a truck and left me here in this shithole with nothing but a dog and an interdimensional alien who went back to his own world when—"

"Spit," he said softly. "Léa . . . look at me."

I shook my head. But he wouldn't let go. He leaned down so he could look me in the eye. "Look at me."

Slowly, I moved my gaze to his face. When he saw I was looking, he angled his head toward the windows, bringing the left side of his face out of shadow. I sucked in a breath so hard that it squeaked.

"Oh, my god," I whispered as my gaze swept over the uneven skin. Except . . . it wasn't as uneven as I remembered. I pulled my hand back, and he finally let go, seeming to sense what I wanted to do. As I laid my fingers against the scar tissue, I shook my head slowly in disbelief.

"My supermodel career is still over," he said with a wry twist of his lips. My gaze drifted up from the scar to the eye that sat above it. There were still some missing eyelashes, but the eye itself was dark and beautiful as it made tiny little movements, examining my face. "But at least I can see now."

I looked at the other eye, situated behind a much prettier set of eyelashes.

"That one doesn't do much," he said. "Except keep

me from freaking people out with an empty eye socket."

"I don't understand."

"Well, you see, there was this psycho bunny who burned my real eye, so I had to go to the vet and get him to remove my eyeball. I didn't even get to wear a cone of shame."

"Not that," I said, my confusion fluttering into something like hope. This guy certainly *sounded* like Viktor. But that was . . . impossible. Wasn't it? "You're dead."

"No, I'm pretty sure I'm alive. If I were dead, I'd be *way* better looking. And I'd have two real eyes. And my left side wouldn't be held together with a few pounds of hardware."

"What?"

He reached up and closed his hand over mine, which was still lingering on his cheek. "I had a bit of an accident."

"C-Roy's runner said you walked in front of a truck."

"Not on purpose. Fart, Léa. Why would I do that?"

I shook my spinning head. "Because you were depressed. And I'd just . . . I'd just forced you to go."

He leaned close, so close that his forehead touched mine. "You did that because you loved me. Remember?"

"I wanted to forget that day so much," I said, my voice choked.

"I'm sorry." He took a deep breath and let out a

sigh. "I'm sorry you thought I was dead. That must've been a bunny."

In spite of the lump in my throat, I had to laugh a little. "You're still Viktor."

"Yeah. I guess so." He straightened up and looked out over the science lab. His gaze fixed on the pile of discarded denim. A small, white dog was curled up on it, head raised and alert. "What the heck happened in here? Did Click Rapture himself?"

"Not exactly." I shook my head again. It still felt like the room was spinning. "He's gone, though."

"So, I guess you have quite a story to tell."

"About what?" I asked, staring at him. It didn't seem real. And yet, there he was, scar and missing eye and all, with just enough differences in the details that I was pretty sure my mind wasn't simply creating him as some sort of survival mechanism. He turned back to me with a frown.

"You okay?" He lifted the back of his hand to my forehead. "You don't *feel* feverish. But you must be really out of it."

"Why?"

"Um . . . haven't you noticed that something's missing?" He removed his hand from my head to wave it out over the room.

"The Rift is gone."

"Yeah, I see that. How?"

"Click." I blew out a long breath. "He wasn't from here. He was from—"

"Reefa."

"That's how he said it."

"Said what?"

"Rift."

He blinked. "You're kidding."

"Nope. He told me all about it. There was some sort of device in his world, and the Rift—" Shaking my head, I sighed. "It's a long story."

"I bet." His lips twitched in a smile. "Now *that* was an exchange student."

"I'll say."

"So he went home?"

I nodded. "He jumped back through. And the Rift closed."

"Oh . . ." he said, in this drawn-out way that made me think a bunch of puzzle pieces had just fallen into place. "You mean that, if someone had just gotten him back to the science lab four years ago, we could've—"

"Yeah," I said quickly, cutting him off. "None of this would've ever happened. Things could've been different."

"They would've been," he said slowly. "But not necessarily in a good way." He reached out and tucked a strand of hair behind my ear. "I probably wouldn't have met you."

"You wouldn't have burned your face. Or lost your eye."

"Eh." He shrugged. "You're worth it."

"Oh, my god, Viktor. Shut—" I stopped myself from finishing the command just in time. "Don't."

"Don't what?"

"Don't shut up. I want to hear every stupid thing that comes out of your mouth."

A wicked amusement danced behind the lenses of his glasses. "Every stupid thing?"

I didn't want to tell him to shut up again. So I just stopped his mouth with a kiss. And that was when I knew he was real. That I wasn't just making him up. Because in all the months we'd been apart, I had never once managed to feel the way I felt at that moment:

Happy.

Safe.

Loved.

"Fart," he whispered as he pulled away. "If I'd known *that* was waiting for me, I would've tried to heal faster." He regarded me with a soft look, then let out a determined-sounding sigh. "So, you ready to get out of the Zone?"

"Out of the Zone," I repeated with a frown. "How did you get *in?*"

"Same way as last time." He held out his right hand. I figured he wanted me to take it, so I did, letting him lead me toward the door. "Buddy! Let's go." A moment later, the dog stood up and shook himself out. The sound of nails on the hard floor followed closely in our wake. There was a lot more light to see by at this hour, at least until we got to the stairwell.

But Viktor pulled a phone from his pocket and turned on the flash, illuminating our path. "Okay. So, I was having a friendly, four-hour chat with Doc Frazier."

"As one does," I said.

He grunted in amusement. "We had a lot to catch up on." He lifted the light higher, shining it down the stairwell. "Here. Mind holding this? I really should use the railing." He handed me the phone, then reached for the metal railing with his free hand as we started to descend.

"Are you okay?" I asked as he grunted his way down the stairs. When we reached the landing, he let out the rest of his breath.

"For now. I've still got another surgery coming up."

"Why?"

"That's kind of what happens with a comminuted femur fracture." He stopped talking as we started down the next set of stairs. Buddy waited for us at the bottom. When we reached him, Viktor held out his hand for the phone, so I passed it over. "It's fine. I'm just glad Aunt Marlena didn't let the docs lop off my leg like they wanted to."

I turned to him, aghast, but since his artificial eye was facing me, he didn't notice. "So you're *not* okay."

"Sure, I am. What? Do I not look okay?" He paused and turned the phone's light on his face. "I even managed to grow a moustache. But Ramona said I looked like a prawn star—"

"A *prawn* star?"

"Yeah. So I shaved it off. But I can still rock a five o'clock shadow."

"Very nice," I said, peering at the faintest dark stubble on his upper lip that I could barely make out in the dim light.

"I think so." Turning the phone back to the floor in front of us, he started forward, still holding my hand. His gait was a little uneven. It wasn't quite a limp, but he wasn't really walking smoothly, either. Our footsteps echoed down the empty hallway as we made our way back to the door.

"How did you know I was here?" I asked as we passed the glass cases.

"I didn't. Not until I got back."

I shook my head. "I think you're telling this story wrong. How did you get back into the Zone?"

"Oh, right. Well, I was having that chat with Doc Frazier, and she was filling me in on a few things."

"I'm surprised she still has a job after what she did for us."

"So is she. But I guess it's hard to find docs who are willing to work here."

"She's military. It's not like she had much of a choice."

He shrugged. We'd reached the corner, so he angled the phone down the hallway to our left and pulled me in that direction. "Anyway, we were just chilling in her little trailer when there was an *awful* lot of activity outside. Not panic, really. Just a bunch of voices. And then someone came and told her she had to see what was going on."

"What *was* going on?"

"Apparently, someone had just turned off the Rift."

I frowned. "How did they even know?"

"They've got cameras trained on the school. And those cameras caught a couple of people sneaking in just minutes before the Rift disappeared. The doc recognized you and Click when she saw the footage. So she sent me in to rescue you."

"Rescue us from what?" I asked. "There's no need for the wall anymore, right? So . . ."

"It'll probably take a while to get everyone out. Lots of paperwork, you see."

"Right."

"I'm assuming." He stopped in front of the door that led outside. "Mind getting that?"

"Is the big guy still out there?"

"Who? The giant?"

"Yeah. He let you in?"

He laughed. "You think I would've gotten in here if he'd tried to block me?"

"No, but—"

"I told him about the Rift. He didn't believe me at first, but then I told him to whip out the hand farts."

"And he couldn't," I guessed.

"Nope. So he went running off."

"Great." The word came out in a groan.

"What?"

"He's one of P-Marc's guys."

"P-Marc?"

"Yeah. That's Permanent Marc's cult leader name. Or something."

"Just as well. 'Permanent Marc' always sounded too much like what you'd find in someone's undies."

"That's a skidmark."

"My point stands. Although . . . P-Marc—"

"Yeah. I know."

He snickered softly.

I shook my head. "His stupid name doesn't matter. We've got bigger problems. He's built up this whole thing around the Rift. The Rosy Dawn. Whatever."

"What?" The word was almost a laugh.

"That's what he calls it. And he calls it 'her.' And he named his cult the Children of the Rosy Dawn."

"Huh. I never knew he was *that* batspit."

"He probably wasn't when you knew him."

"He was sticking a bent paperclip into an electrical outlet. It's debatable."

My eyes widened. "Is that what caused the Rift?"

"No. It was Cody's science project."

I thought about what Click had drawn. The two towers and the Rift stretching between them. "All it needed was a spark," I muttered.

"What?"

"Maybe your project had something to do with it. But if Marc hadn't been messing around . . ."

He sighed. "Whatever it was, it's gone now."

"Yeah, and Marc's going to be pissed. It was like . . . his baby. He thinks he created it. So now he's going to think I killed his baby."

"So what do you want to do? Is there somewhere we can go and hide out until nightfall?" He paused, seeming to think. "Where have you been living?"

"In my old house. But it's in Marc's territory. And he knows I live there. It's not safe."

"Then we'll just have to go now."

"Go where?"

He let out a grunt of amused disbelief. "Out."

"Out of the Zone?"

"Yeah. Why not?"

"And where do you propose I go? I don't have anyone on the outside, remember? Everyone I had . . ."

"What?" he asked gently.

"They're gone. Dead."

"I'm sorry."

"Where am I going to go? Niesha's parents didn't have room for me, and—"

"You're coming home with me."

"Viktor, I can't do that forever."

"Why not? Aunt Marlena and Uncle Craig are fine with it."

"Did you ask them?"

"They *will* be fine with it."

I sighed. "I'm not going to force my way into their lives. That's not fair to them. Or to Ramona. Or to you."

"But I want you in my life."

"It's not your house."

"Okay, then, if they say no, we'll get our own place."

I snorted. "You're too young to get your own place."

"Um, excuse me. I'm nineteen." He paused. "Okay, officially, I'm eighteen, but if it's a maturity thing . . ."

"Do you really want me to finish that thought?"

"Do I?" he asked innocently. I sighed and turned to the door, ready to push on the handle. But he squeezed my hand.

"Let's just get out of here. We can figure out all the details later. Okay?"

"Okay," I said. I wanted to protest some more, but I had a feeling I wasn't going to win any arguments. It was easier to just go with it and deal with any potential issues later, once we were safely away from the Zone. So I pushed on the door. Early-morning sunlight leaked inside, making me squint. Viktor let go of my hand so he could step out. As I peered through the open doorway, I saw that the lawn chair was empty.

Buddy ran outside and went straight for the corner of the building where a tangle of weeds was growing, lifting his leg and releasing an impressive amount of pee on the wall. Viktor chuckled as he watched, absently slipping his phone back into his pocket. I stepped out of the school, letting the door swing shut behind me. When I looked up, the sky was clear. The clouds from the night before were gone, and above us stretched the deep, featureless blue of a March sky.

"Hard to believe it's been four years," Viktor said. I turned to him with a frown.

"Really? An awful lot has happened."

"Isn't time supposed to fly faster for older folks?"

"Older folks?" I repeated, watching as a cheeky smile spread over his face. I stepped toward him, getting a better look in the daylight. His skin was a much nicer colour than the last time I'd seen him. Less sallow. More . . . alive.

"Can't stop looking at my handsome face, eh?"

"What happened to your scar?"

"A few thousand dollars worth of laser treatments." He turned his head from side to side, striking the pose of a flamboyant model. "How do I look?"

"Pretty good, actually."

He laughed, taken aback. "'Actually'?"

"Your eye."

"I kind of wanted to get a patch and just do the pirate thing, but Aunt Marlena wasn't putting up with that." He readjusted his glasses with one hand, then looked over at Buddy, who'd finally finished peeing and was examining the saggy lawn chair. "I guess we've got a dog."

"I guess."

"Click didn't want to take him?"

I shook my head. "We were trying to restore balance."

He didn't ask any more questions about that. He

just smiled and tilted his head toward the fencing where the twinkle lights glowed dimly, almost invisible in the morning light.

"Let's get out of this farting heckhole."

—

I knew enough about the neighbourhood to the north of the school to know that it was a tangle of cul-de-sacs and looping crescents. I wasn't sure if any of them emptied onto the road we needed to reach the checkpoint, though, so we headed back to Addervine Way, the street that ran in front of the high school. The one that cut right through Marc's territory. I stayed close to Viktor's right side, scanning the area like a frightened squirrel as Buddy trotted ahead of us, looking back periodically to make sure we were following.

The walk seemed to take forever. I couldn't remember how long it had taken the last time. That time, though, I'd been holding Viktor's hand. This time, I didn't dare. Not because of what he might think, but because I didn't want to give Marc any excuse to take out his rage on the wrong person if he happened to catch up to us. I didn't know how likely that was. The territory seemed oddly quiet. Then again, it had been quiet the last time, too. And now it was a Wednesday, just hours away from a cult meeting.

My new reality didn't seem real. Every once in a

while, I would reach out and brush my fingers over Viktor's sleeve just to hear the very real sound of skin on nylon, or I'd poke him in the shoulder to judge his solidity. The first couple of times I did it, he turned to look at me, his mouth twitching in amusement. Finally, though, seemingly sick of being poked, he grabbed my hand and held it tight. Since I hadn't heard anything in ages—voices, footsteps, or any other signs of life—I didn't pull away.

"I'm real," he said as we passed out of the densest area of Marc's territory. Up ahead, I could see part of the wall.

"I thought you were dead for six months."

"I thought I was dead for the first few." He tilted his face toward the sky and smiled. The limp was getting a little more pronounced as we walked on. "Feels *so* good to see something above me other than a ceiling."

"Viktor," I said hesitantly, not sure if I wanted to hear the answer, "what were you planning to do?"

"About what?"

"When you came back. You said you only found out about the Rift when you were already talking to Dr. Frazier."

He turned to look down at me. "What do you think I was doing?"

"Coming back into the Zone. But that would've been *really* stupid."

"Why?"

I let out a cough of disbelief. "Is there something wrong with your memory?"

"Nope. I remembered that I had friends in here. And they needed me." He squeezed my hand. "And I needed them."

"Surely you have friends on the outside."

He shrugged. "Not really. Aside from Niesha, I mean."

"You keep in touch?"

"We were the only two Rifters who'd gotten out. And we've been keeping it quiet."

"Didn't the hospital notice they were treating a teenager from Kenyonville?"

"Oh, yeah. And a lot of them were weird about it. Too quiet. Either that, or they wanted to know what was going on in here. A lot of people are missing their kids."

"What did you tell them?"

He shook his head. "Nothing. What could I have said? They saw me with their own eyes. Not much I could've done to paint *that* turd with glitter."

I snorted. "Nice."

"Everyone will be getting out in a few days, anyway."

"Not everyone." I looked down at Buddy, at his tail that was bouncing jauntily. He seemed to be in a good mood. Maybe he sensed that we were going to a place where he'd never have to be hungry again. A land of milk and . . . kibble.

"True. Cody's gone."

I shook my head. "I'm talking about people who actually died."

"Your grandparents?" he asked. I looked at him in surprise. "We do have the internet out there, Léa."

"Yeah, but—"

"I found your grandmother's obituary. You and your grandfather were both named in it."

"I remember."

"And since you were hanging out with C-Roy for a while before you met us, I figured your grandfather must have died at some point, too."

"You figured right."

"Why didn't you tell me?"

"Because I didn't want to think about it."

He was silent for a few moments. "Léa," he said at last, "what happened?"

"Marc killed him."

"Son of a bunny."

"Maybe it was one of his goons. I don't know. He never said. But—"

"Fart, Léa. It doesn't matter who did it." He came to a sudden stop. I wasn't sure what he was doing . . . until I found myself wrapped in his arms. A few months earlier, my first instinct would've been to pull away. Instead, I burst into tears. Body-heaving ones that I was glad nobody else was around to see. Strangely, though, I didn't care that he was there to witness them. "I've got you," he whispered. "You're all right."

I believed him.

I held on tight, clamping my fists around handfuls of his jacket as we stood there in the fresh morning. This was what I had wanted for so many months, even as I'd believed it wasn't possible. My body shook with sobs as I tried to keep them quiet, and all the while, he just held me. Even when the hug got awkwardly long. Reluctantly, I let go of him. But he kept his arms where they were.

"It's okay," he said. "You're not done yet."

In spite of the sobs that were still stuck in my throat, I managed to get out a tiny laugh. "What?"

"One thing I learned in the past few months is that letting your feelings out is a good thing."

I sniffed. "That's not *my* thing."

"I know," he said. But he still didn't let go. So I put my arms back around him and took a few deep breaths. The tightness in my throat started to ease. "Just so you know," he said, "I cried over being parted from you, even if you didn't cry over being parted from me."

The snort that erupted out of me sounded disgustingly juicy. I tried to pull away again, and this time he let me. Wiping my cheeks, I stared up at him. "You're still Viktor."

"At your service." He gave me a little bow before grabbing my hand and starting to walk again, a little faster this time, even though that seemed to make the limp worse. "Come on. You've been in this heckhole long enough."

"You think?"

"What's the first thing you want to do when you get out? Want to see a movie? Get a ridiculously expensive coffee? Have dinner?"

"Those all sound suspiciously like dates."

"Yeah. So?"

I laughed as my cheeks got warm. "I was thinking about a really long bath. Followed by a really long nap."

He made a dismissive noise that sounded almost like one of his raspberries. "You got boring since I left."

"Really? Has your life been that exciting out there?"

"Not unless you call physio and doc appointments exciting." He walked a few more steps in silence, then shook his head. "All I really wanted was to be here with you. No matter how boring that was."

"Well, for all you knew, you could've gotten your wish. What would you have done if the Rift *hadn't* closed?"

"Marital bliss with my bestie for the next seventy years?"

"Marital bliss." I snorted. "First of all, you haven't asked me to do anything."

"Getting down on one knee is kind of hard these days, so—"

"Second, who was going to marry us?"

"Good point. I guess we would've had to just shack up together."

"I was not about to shack up with anyone in here. There's no birth control, and the last thing the Rift

Zone needed was another inmate." I stared down at the ground as we walked. "Besides," I said quietly, "I'm not sure if I want to have kids."

"Why?" he asked. There was no judgement in his tone. Just simple curiosity.

"After seeing how people can treat each other . . . After seeing how the world can treat a bunch of innocent kids . . ."

"Okay. Yeah. I get that." He squeezed my hand. "I guess the RZRA isn't really necessary anymore, is it?"

"That," I said, "was never going to happen, anyway."

He grunted in amusement. We continued to walk, getting closer and closer to the checkpoint. The road curved a little bit, and then we could see the gate, an opening that beckoned to us in the bright day. For some reason, the hastily constructed wall—complete with its view-blocking panels and razor wire—didn't seem so ominous anymore. Maybe because it was no longer necessary. Or maybe the hope that was riding like a balloon in the middle of my chest was making me a little loopy.

But that hope popped suddenly with a sharp report that echoed through the air around us. Instinctively, I ducked into a crouch, pulling my hand out of Viktor's as I curled my arms and legs into myself. Buddy, startled by the noise, broke into a run and skittered ahead of us.

"Fart," Viktor said as he looked back. "Fart, fart, fart."

"What?" My heart was pounding so hard that my whole body was bouncing. Slowly, I turned, the balls of my feet scraping on the gritty road. When I saw the figure, I stood up. Fast.

"What did you do?" Marc shouted. He lowered his arm—which had been pointing straight up in the air—and aimed the gun directly at me. "What did you fucking do?"

"Does it look like she did anything?" Viktor asked, waving his hand at me.

"Shut up, Cody."

"I think you have me confused with—"

"No, I don't. Don't pull that bullshit with me." He shook the gun in my direction, almost like he was trying to make it manually release bullets. "You went into the school. The Rosy Dawn died. And now you're out here. So you better start talking, or—"

"Or what?" Viktor asked. "You going to shoot her?"

I squeaked as the gun swung to point at him. Marc was maybe fifty feet away. Too far to get an accurate shot (I hoped), but way too close for comfort.

"Don't hurt him," I said, my voice small.

"What?"

"Don't hurt him!" My voice carried down the street. We were close enough to the wall that there was an odd echo.

"Why shouldn't I? He's helping a murderer."

"Spit," Viktor whispered, leaning a little closer to me so he could keep his voice down. "Who'd you kill, Léa?"

"I didn't kill your precious Rosy Dawn," I called across the space. "She . . . needed help."

Marc's eyes went wide. I knew I'd said the wrong thing, but I wasn't sure why it was the wrong thing.

"Run," Viktor whispered. "Toward the checkpoint."

I resisted the urge to look at him. Marc was standing there, sides heaving, as he seemed to build with rage. The gun's muzzle swung back in my direction.

"He's going to shoot me," I said.

"He can try. It's hard to hit a moving target. Run. Zigzag if you have to."

"Can *you* run?"

"I sure hope so."

That was probably the least reassuring thing he could've said at that moment. I took a step backward. Marc's head twitched, causing his locs to sway. I turned and ran.

I expected bullets to start flying right away. But all I could hear were my footsteps. And then another set, right beside me. Or, sort of beside me. Viktor seemed to be keeping his distance. That was probably wise. We didn't want to make a bigger target for the guy with the gun.

Buddy, who had been halfway to the checkpoint, saw us coming and ran in a wide circle, unsure what to do. As soon as we got close, though, he seemed to understand that we were running for our lives, and he took off in the right direction, pumping his little legs as he sprinted toward safety. I kept my focus on him so I wouldn't think about what was behind us.

But that became very hard to do when the first shot rang out.

Viktor grunted, and then he wasn't beside me anymore. I skidded to a stop and looked back to see him pushing himself up from the ground. My vision focused to a fine point as it scanned his body, looking for the problem. The dark stain spreading through his jeans on his lower right leg was a sight that sent me into a panic.

"Viktor?"

He looked up at me, an expression of terror in his eyes as he saw me standing there. "Run. Run!"

I couldn't. I stepped toward him instead. But I didn't get far before the second shot rang out. I sucked in a breath, wobbling on my feet as what felt like a punch slammed into my right shoulder.

"No." Viktor staggered to his feet and limped toward me, looking like a crazed zombie. "Léa, run!"

I just stood there, staring at the former cult leader who was marching toward us, a sick little smirk on his lips, the gun still levelled at me. My body seemed frozen, and I couldn't move. I didn't feel any pain, either, which didn't make sense. *Did I just get shot? I think I just got shot. Why doesn't it hurt?* But I didn't have long to think about any of that because Viktor reached me, grabbed my hand, and nearly yanked me off my feet as he spun me toward the checkpoint. Somehow, I managed to make my feet move.

Beyond the sound of my heart hammering in my

ears, I could hear a dog barking and voices shouting. I didn't think those voices were Viktor or Marc, though. They were coming from up ahead. Through streaming eyes, I saw the figures bunch into the checkpoint gate, creating an impenetrable wall of camo and rifles. A sob escaped me as all my hopes crashed into my nine toes.

"Lower your weapon!" a deep voice shouted. I thought the man was talking to me, and it didn't make any sense because my hands weren't glowing and they weren't raised at all. One was clasped tightly in Viktor's, and the other one was . . . I wasn't sure. My arm seemed to be going numb.

"Stop that fucking murderer!" Marc screamed. The terrifying fury in his voice spurred me to run even faster, toward the wall of really big guns that were pointing straight at us. "Stop them!"

"Lower your—" The end of the command was swallowed by a single shot. My legs buckled, and I crashed face first to the ground, landing half on my shoulder, half on the side of my head, skidding into the asphalt with so much friction that I was certain Viktor and I were going to have matching facial scars. But I didn't have time for more than that first thought as a deafening clatter erupted above our heads, and Viktor threw his entire body over mine. As the crushing weight pressed my body into the hard street, things *finally* started to hurt. I let out a strangled, sobbing scream.

The haze of pain swallowed me. All I could hear were my own whimpering breaths. My ears were still vibrating, causing all the other sounds to cut in and out. But I could feel the ground thump and shake. And Viktor's body, on top of me, pressed down with a terrifying, dead weight.

"No," I sobbed. "Viktor! Viktor!" My screams were weak with grief and disappointment and pain. After everything we'd gone through, for it to end like—

"Shh." The sound was almost lost through the hissing in my ears. The weight lifted as Viktor slid off me, brightening the world once more. I blinked, looking into his concerned face just inches away from mine. He brushed back my hair so I could see him better. "You're all right, Léa. You're all right."

"You're not!" I wailed, and I started to cry. Each sob was like a blow from a knife, driving itself into my torso. "It's not fair. You never should have come back. Now you—"

"I'm fine, okay?"

"You got shot!"

He glanced up at something behind me, then turned his gaze back to my face. "Doc Frazier's here. She's going to—"

"He got shot!" I shouted. "Don't let him die. Please, don't let him die."

"Léa." A familiar female voice came from behind me. "Viktor's fine, all right? It's just a flesh wound. But we'll check him out." Something touched the back of my right leg, and I flinched. "Sorry. I'm going to need to apply some pressure here."

"Where?" I mumbled.

"Sorry to have to tell you this," Viktor said, "but you've been shot in the butt."

"What?"

"Technically, it's her upper leg," Dr. Frazier said.

"That won't be any fun when we tell this story later." Viktor gave me a weak smile. I couldn't return it.

There seemed to be a lot of activity going on around us. There were other voices, and I could see more figures out of the corner of my eye. I groped my hand across the gritty pavement between us. Viktor grasped it in his and brought it to his lips. I closed my eyes.

"Hey, Léa, stay with me. You won't want to miss this next part."

"What part?" I mumbled.

"Getting out of here. This is just the beginning."

"Yeah?"

"Yeah." He squeezed my hand and gave it a little shake. "Come on, Léa. Open your eyes."

"I can't breathe."

"I know, Léa," Dr. Frazier said. Her voice seemed to rise as she spoke. "Just try to relax, all right? Chaudhary, help me. Let's get her on her back. Viktor, I need you to move out of the way for a sec."

The cold absence as Viktor slipped his fingers out of mine was almost too much to bear. I kept my eyes tightly shut as the world flipped and spun in slow motion, making me dizzy even with the steadying set of hands on my head. My next attempt to take a deep breath failed, and all I managed to suck in was a pathetic wheeze.

"Léa," Viktor whispered. A soft hand brushed my cheek, and I pulled my eyelids open. He hovered at my right, his different-but-familiar face like an anchor. An unfamiliar young man in scrubs crouched attentively behind him. Dr. Frazier knelt on my left, a pair of steel scissors flashing in her hand as she cut through my shirt. *Thank god I'm wearing a bra.*

"I don't want to die," I said. The doctor nodded before turning away to grab a plastic packet and tearing it open.

"Then let's make sure you don't." She pressed something soft against my right shoulder, just above my bra. "Let's get you out of here and into a proper hospital. Let's get your life back. All right?"

I blinked at her, not really understanding. "You're not going to treat me?"

"I don't have to. Not anymore." She paused, seeming to listen. I listened, too. It was a few moments before I heard it, way off in the distance. It wasn't an uncommon sound. We'd heard it occasionally in the Zone. But now . . . it was coming closer. Now . . . it heralded hope.

Viktor stared at the doctor. "Is that an ambulance? How'd it get here so fast?"

"They've been on standby since last night," Dr. Frazier said. "On my orders. The evacuation starts today. And the first ride out is for you, Léa. Congratulations. You'll be the first to leave the Rift Zone."

"Not actually the first," Viktor pointed out.

"Officially." She looked down at my face and gave me a gentle smile. "Whatever you did . . . thank you. On behalf of all those who have been trapped in there for the last four years."

"I didn't . . ."

"I bet you did, Léa," Viktor said. I swivelled my aching eyeballs in his direction. "Click couldn't have done it without you. We all needed each other in there. It doesn't matter how much or how little. We had to stick together, and we had to make things work. Heck, I wouldn't even be here if it wasn't for you. So . . . yeah. Thank you."

I waited for him to say something else, to end on a joke. But he didn't. He just leaned down and kissed my forehead. His lips felt hot. But maybe I was just cold.

He lay down again and snuggled up close to my side, and we lay there in silence as the siren drew closer. The sky stretched overhead, a brilliant blue unmarked by even a single cloud. *A blank slate*, I thought.

And despite the pain and uncertainty that I knew was barrelling toward me . . . I couldn't wait to start writing on it.

CHAPTER 17

THAT HAS A NICE RING TO IT

The little white dog sat on the grass, head cocked to one side as he listened to the child give the command. But I knew he was just waiting for the treat that was sure to come out of that tiny fist.

"Come on, Buddy," Viktor said, propped up on his elbows beside the crouching toddler. "Dance. You can do it."

"Isn't that dog getting kind of old for that?" Craig asked from the table as he set a refill of lemonade in front of Katja.

"He's not too old to do tricks," Viktor said. "Especially if there's food involved." He pushed his glasses back up his nose, then turned to the little boy. "Tell him again."

"Dance!" Carrick cried. The command finally seemed to register in Buddy's tiny brain, and he stood up on his hind legs, tail whipping as he tried to keep his balance. Carrick squealed in delight. "He did it!"

"He did. Now give him his treat so he knows he did a good job."

Carrick offered the scrap of roast chicken, and Buddy's dance stopped abruptly. He horked down the morsel, then licked the boy's hand for good measure. Carrick dissolved into giggles, which made the adults at the table laugh.

"Okay," Niesha said. "That's enough treats for now. You'll make Uncle Viktor's dog sick."

Carrick didn't seem to have heard her. He patted Buddy's head. The dog tried to sniff his hand, searching for more treats.

"It would take a lot more than that to make him sick," Viktor said as he stood up. He watched the boy and the dog for a moment, then scooped the former off the ground. "Léa fed him Cheeznudle casserole for months."

"I did not," I said, casting a quick glance at Dr. Bryan a few places from me down the table. But he just shook his head with a smile, seeming to realize that Viktor was joking. "I just didn't force him to eat pine trees. Unlike some people."

"Jesus," Niesha said. "I can't even imagine." She stabbed at the remains of cake on her plate.

"Things got bad after you left," Viktor said, plunking Carrick on her lap. The little boy, spying the last bit of cake, immediately tried to grab it. She lifted the fork up out of reach.

"Please!"

"You already had dessert. Doesn't Mama get any?"

He grunted and tugged at her arm. She quickly pushed the bite into her mouth and set the fork down.

"All gone."

Turning to Katja, he scowled. "Mommy! Mama ate it!"

"I know she did. But you already had yours, okay?"

He shook his head. Niesha rolled her eyes.

"Speaking of things getting bad," she said, trying to settle the squirming two-year-old on her lap, "is there any news about the settlement?"

"Nothing definitive yet," Marlena said. "Frankly, I'm surprised the suit has progressed as fast as it has. Five years isn't very long, in the grand scheme of things."

"It's 'cause you're an awesome lawyer," Viktor said, re-taking his seat beside me. In the lights hanging above us in the summer twilight, the shiny scar on his right calf almost seemed to glow. "They should've thought twice before imprisoning the nephew of one of the country's most—"

"Okay, okay. Flattery will get you nowhere, mister."

"Really? Huh. Seems to work okay most of the time."

She shot him a look. He just grinned and leaned back in his chair.

"I don't know how anything could ever be enough," Dr. Bryan said. "After everything that happened to you kids in there."

"I agree," Craig said. He cast a quick glance at Ramona, who was slumped in her chair, absorbed with her phone. "As soon as the military knew about the proximity thing, everyone should've been released."

"That's the sticking point," Marlena said. "Getting hold of those records of what they knew and when they knew it."

"They knew for at least half a year before we got out the first time," Viktor said. "Doc Frazier said she suspected that being close to the Rift was the problem. And we proved that when we left."

"I don't think they wanted to believe it," Niesha said, shaking her head. Viktor snorted.

"You think they *wanted* to keep us in there?"

"Maybe. They liked having a whole cage of guinea pigs."

"It was a pretty good psychological experiment," Katja said, reaching for Carrick and pulling him onto her lap. He looked like he was about to fall asleep in that sudden way toddlers do. "I'm surprised they didn't start asking us to come in to give blood."

"Or pee in a cup," Viktor added.

"I'm not sure if anything would've shown up on any tests," Dr. Bryan said. "Not from a toxicological standpoint, anyway. From what I've heard, the Rift was an electromagnetic phenomenon that took advantage of the physiology of people of a certain age."

Craig raised an eyebrow. "You make it sound like it knew what it was doing."

The vet shrugged. "Perhaps it did. I suppose we'll never know. There are a lot of things we'll never know."

Craig and Dr. Bryan continued to speculate about the Rift. Marlena asked Katja if she wanted to put Carrick down for a nap in the house, which led to an exchange about how jealous adults were of toddler sleep habits. Ramona seemed to be checked out completely. As I tipped the last of my lemonade into my mouth and set down the glass of half-melted ice cubes, Viktor turned to me and waggled his eyebrows. When I gave my head a quick shake, he leaned close so he could whisper in my ear. "Now?"

"Maybe we shouldn't."

"Why not? Aren't you proud of it?"

I shrugged.

"It's something to be proud of."

"Your name's on it, too."

"So? Does that mean I can't think it's awesome?"

I snorted. We'd had a variation on the conversation many times over the previous few months. "You think it's awesome because it was your idea."

"It's a great idea."

"And you really want all your worst moments out there for the world to see?"

He tipped his head back, looking haughty and corny all at once. "Those moments make me tragically, vulnerably relatable."

"Thank you for reminding me why I did most of it."

"I'm your muse."

"Whatever, smartass."

He grinned. "See? You can't deny it." He nudged me in the shoulder. "Go on. Get it."

"Get it yourself. You're perfectly capable."

"So are you."

"My ass still tingles if I walk too much."

"My left leg aches when it rains. My right leg aches in the heat. My eye socket—"

"Okay, okay. Jesus," I said, hauling myself to my feet. "It's not a competition."

"No?"

"No." I worked my fingers into his hair as I passed, roughing it up a little. It was longer than when we'd first gotten out of the Zone, but still not long enough to wear in a ponytail. I kind of missed that long hair . . . but I wasn't about to give him styling tips.

As I stepped up to the sliding glass door, Buddy ran over to me. "Stay out here," I said. "You're just going to want to come back out in a minute." But he scratched at the metal frame. As soon as I pulled the door open, he squeezed inside and ran straight for the kitchen, no doubt hoping that someone had dropped a few morsels during meal preparation. I headed downstairs to the basement suite I shared with Viktor.

The object of my trip inside was right where I'd left it, tucked under a stack of t-shirts in our dresser. I pulled it out carefully, a little frisson running through me—just like it had the first time—as I gazed at the cover of the book. It had only been delivered a few days earlier. I still couldn't believe it. And, sometimes, I wasn't sure if I wanted to go through with it. But the whole process had been a good sort of therapy . . . for both of us. I closed the drawer, tucked the book behind me, and walked back upstairs.

Buddy was still in the kitchen, frantically searching for droppings. His nails clicked on the hard floor as he made another circuit of the island. I debated leaving him inside, but I knew he'd probably start to bark if I did that, and then someone would have to let him out again.

"Come on," I said. "Outside." When he didn't respond, I tried again. "Buddy! Outside. Now."

He trotted into view and stopped, tilting his head with a quizzical look. It was hard to be mad at him when he did that. Puppy-dog eyes were a powerful weapon. Dr. Bryan said the dog was probably close to fourteen now. But it seemed that cuteness never died.

"Let's go," I said, and started for the door. A moment later, I heard the clatter of nails on the floor as he ran ahead of me, beating me by a wide margin.

When I emerged onto the patio, things were much as I'd left them. Quiet conversation was still happening—this time with Ramona having deigned to talk to Niesha and Katja—but Viktor seemed to be waiting for me. I saw his gaze drift to the arm I was holding behind my back, and his face lit up in a smile. He stood, which immediately made me want to throw the book at him and run inside. Which was ridiculous. But, still.

"Family and friends," he said, his commanding voice putting an immediate stop to all the other conversations. Ramona snorted. Niesha rolled her eyes. Marlena shook her head. When Viktor saw that he had everyone's attention, he swept his hand dramatically toward me. "Behold!"

"Behold what, dumbass?" Ramona muttered. Craig shot her a warning look.

"Léa and I," Viktor said, choosing to ignore his sister, "are about to bring something into the world that—"

Niesha gasped. "Oh, my god."

He turned to her in confusion. "Huh?"

"He better not have," Ramona said. "They're not even married."

It took a moment for me to realize what she was talking about. What they were probably all thinking. Viktor seemed to get it at the same moment I did. He quickly shook his head.

"No, I . . . That's not it. I mean—"

"I'm not pregnant," I said, saving him from his adorable fluster. "The RZRA is off the table."

"The what?" Craig asked.

"You don't want to know," Niesha said. She turned back to Viktor. "If it's not a baby, then . . ."

"Ta-da!" Viktor said, with a dramatic swoop of his

arm in my direction. I just stood there like an idiot. He laughed. "That's your cue, Léa."

"Oh. Right." I slipped the thick volume out from behind my back and held it up in both hands so everyone could see it. The backyard fell silent. And it remained silent for so long that I began to worry that something was very wrong. But then . . .

"Awesome," Ramona said. She was actually smiling. "I'm guessing you wrote most of it, though, because Viktor's a moron."

"Hey!"

"*Generation Rift* by Léa Young and Viktor Knowles," Dr. Bryan read. "Very impressive."

"That's not going to interfere with the settlement, is it?" Niesha asked, casting a quick, worried glance at Marlena. But before she could say anything, Viktor shook his head.

"Nope. We checked with our lawyer. Léa was worried about the same thing." He held up his hands. "It's all fine. Besides, it's technically fiction. Even if it's based on fact."

"Post-apocalyptic?" Katja said.

"Post-apocalyptic *romance*," he corrected her.

"Viktor's idea," I said quickly, which made almost everyone laugh. Including him.

"It's definitely enemies to lovers," he said as he walked over to me and peered at the cover. "Why is everything so blue again?"

"Because I had to change the colour of the Rift energy, remember?"

"Right . . . 'cause 'blueballs' is so much better than 'pinkballs.' I remember now."

Dr. Bryan shook his head. "How much of this book did you actually write, Viktor?"

"As in . . . how many words did I physically etch onto a piece of parchment with a quill and my own blood?"

"Zero," I said. "And the same goes for me. I used a laptop." I turned to Viktor, who was looking amused. "But we came up with the plot together."

"And the characters."

"Why fiction?" Niesha asked. It was probably what they all wanted to know. I bit my lip as I looked at Viktor. The real reason wasn't anything we could share. I wasn't even supposed to know about Viktor's former identity. There were only five people in that backyard who knew the truth, and it would have to stay that way.

"Well," Viktor began, "the reading public couldn't handle all my awesomeness."

"Sure," Niesha said, a smirk crossing her features.

"It's true! Plus, we didn't want to out C-Roy as a foot freak and Rasputin as a couple of batspit psychos. We all had to do things in there that we aren't proud of."

Katja's expression darkened. "Viktor, Rasputin caused you to lose your eye. You don't owe them anything."

He glanced at me. "It just . . . wouldn't have felt right. They lost a lot, too."

"Everyone did," Craig said. "And I'm proud of the way you kids handled it."

"We couldn't have done it alone," Viktor said, turning to Dr. Bryan. "It was good to have allies."

"I'm glad I could help." Dr. Bryan raised his half-empty glass. "But I really think we need to celebrate the people who were affected the most. The ones who survived."

"And the ones who didn't," Niesha said quietly, reaching over to stroke her fingers through her son's curls. Carrick slept on, oblivious to the tribute to his namesake.

Those who could reach a glass raised theirs, holding them high in the air. "To Generation Rift," Dr. Bryan said.

"To Generation Rift," voices echoed around the table. I just stood there, holding the book and feeling a gentle warmth spreading through my chest. I looked at Viktor, only to find him watching me with a strange look in his dark eyes. He smiled, shook his head, and stuck his hand into the pocket of his shorts.

"Okay," he said. "Well. Um. I don't know how to say this."

"That's a first," Ramona muttered. "Spit it out!"

He shot her a dark look, then turned back to me. With his free hand, he took the book and placed it on the table before taking my hand and leading me a few steps away to where the suspended lights created a canopy of illumination. Buddy followed, seeming to think there was going to be food involved. He sat down and looked up at us eagerly.

"What are you doing?" I asked, my voice suspicious. "This is weird behaviour. Even for you."

He smiled nervously. Then he took a deep breath as he pulled his hand from his pocket. I saw a flash just as someone—possibly Ramona—stifled a little squeal.

"I'd get down on one knee if I could," he began, holding the ring between us. I just stared at it, feeling my eyes get wider and wider. "But it's not a good idea for me to kneel on concrete, and if I have to drag you over to the grass now, it'll ruin the mood. So . . ."

I looked up into his eyes. I could barely see them past the reflections in his glasses. But what I *could* see was an expression of affection. Of hope. And, weirdly, of fear.

"Viktor—"

"Before you say no, can I just—"

"Who says I'm saying no?"

"You're saying yes?"

I laughed. "Are you going to let me say anything?"

"Right. Sorry." He shook his head. "I better ask properly if I want a proper answer. Right?"

"Right."

"Okay." He straightened up a little as if to brace himself for whatever was coming. "Léa Rosalie Young, BFF and co-author, Cheeznudle critic and dendrophobe—"

"What?"

"It's someone with a fear of trees."

"Huh?"

"You bunnied about eating pine needles for weeks."

I shook my head, trying to hold in a laugh. "Get to the point, Viktor."

"Right. Léa Rosalie Young, will you be my wife and *not* do the RZRA with me?"

"That," I said, "is probably the weirdest proposal I've ever heard."

"What else did you expect from him?" Ramona called from the table before her mother discreetly shushed her.

"Nothing," I said, shaking my head slowly. "I wouldn't expect anything else. And I wouldn't *want* anything else." I looked up into his eyes again, only to see that the expression there had changed. "Yes," I said, watching as the smile bloomed on his uneven face. "Yes, Viktor. I will marry you."

The table erupted in applause as he slipped the ring onto my shaking finger with equally shaking ones of his own. I reached up and steadied my hands on his face, leaning forward to kiss him. Out of the corner of my eye, I saw him pump his fist in the air. I pulled away, eyebrow raised.

"I got myself a cougar!" he said, addressing our friends and family.

"Jesus, Viktor," Niesha said as the table erupted in laughter. "Don't make her regret it."

My hands were still on his face, so I turned his

head back toward me. "You're plenty legal now, young man. Besides . . . I plan on living a long time. So I need someone who's not going to die first and leave me as a widow."

"Good point. You'd be lost without me."

He was just joking.

But they were probably the truest words he'd ever spoken.

ALSO BY
NISSA HARLOW

Two Between Worlds
The Last Minute
No Such Thing
Elements of Mind: The Complete Quartet

Generation Rift
Nothing Close to Home
Escape From the Zone
So Lost Are the Foes
All the Scars of Hope

ABOUT
THE AUTHOR

Nissa Harlow wanted to be a writer from the time she was a small child, but it took a while before she finally did anything about it. In the meantime, she worked as a volunteer day-camp counsellor, a movie extra, and a digital-photo editor. She even once worked on a conveyor belt in a chocolate factory (which was as stressful—and delicious—as it sounds).

These days, she lives in British Columbia, Canada and writes stories about friendship, love, and healing, all embellished with a touch of the fantastic.